THE WOMAN CALLED BILLY
STOOD UP AND
BEGAN UNDRESSING.

"What do you think you're doing?" asked Raider.

"What does it look like? Ah'm so tired ah can't keep my eyes open..."

"Be a gentleman, Raider," said Doc. "Or make believe you are. Offer the lady a place to sleep."

Raider bristled. "Where am I supposed to?"

Billy leered. "You'h welcome on eithah side o' me..."

"Not 'nough room."

"How 'bout on top?"

J.D. HARDIN

CARNIVAL OF DEATH

BERKLEY BOOKS, NEW YORK

CARNIVAL OF DEATH

A Berkley Book / published by arrangement with
the author

PRINTING HISTORY
Berkley edition / February 1984

ISBN: 0-425-06842-0

PRINTED IN THE UNITED STATES OF AMERICA

CHAPTER ONE

Everything in the office was dark, noted Doc: dark green, brown, black, from the oak-paneled walls to the ancient and wretched-looking ark of a desk to the funereal shade capping the lamp, illuminating its cluttered work space and sending soft shafts of light upward, wide-streaking the walls and ceiling. Outside the grime-encrusted window a streetlight attempted valiantly if unsuccessfully to pierce the misty gloom. The sounds of night in the city blended melodramatically: a bottle shattering, loud arguing, a scream, a dog growling and yipping, the mournful clopping of hooves on cobblestones as a hansom passed. The arguers were joined by a third voice, a woman's, loud and vituperative. Raider, sitting opposite Doc, shifted his bulk uneasily in his chair, his dark eyes flicking left and right.

Sergeant Montaigne was seated at the desk in black alpaca vest and shirt-sleeves that ballooned so, the garters holding his cuffs up and off his pudgy hands were lost to the eye. He was in his fifties, surmised Doc, but looked ten years older, his scalp plastered with thinning strands of pigeon gray hair, his eyes weary and pinched over his spectacles, his appearance altogether harried, as well might be that of any long-time member of the New Orleans police force. Admittedly, the 364 men under Chief David Hennessey's command had to be the most frustrated, overworked, underrewarded, and underpaid law officers in any city in the country. Montaigne's earlier description of New Orleans as "the city that care forgot" appeared appropriate. The devil's backyard might also apply. The proportion of crime to the population of 190,000 was perfectly astounding. In a nutshell, the city was the helpless victim of an ongoing reign of terror so far beyond the capabilities and facilities of the police force to quell or even abate that the mere thought was ridiculous. The criminal element that had created and maintained this hell on earth found refuge and amusement in the groggeries, bordellos, dance halls, and barrel houses crowding the Vieux Carré and the area above Canal Street. In the half dozen blocks between Canal and the City Hall at Lafayette Square alone, there were forty-five places where liquor could be purchased, each more disreputable and dangerous than the one preceding it. Brothels, from the ten-dollar parlor house to the fifteen-cent Negro crib, crammed dozens of blocks. And, except in the outlying parts of the city, there was scarcely a single block that did not boast at least one such establishment.

Montaigne continued his description of "Sodom and Gomorrah on the Delta," skillfully detailing the situation the two visiting Pinkertons could expect to confront.

"The Sicilians come heah befoah the War, settlin' in the Second and Third Districts, mostly. They was counterfeiters, burglars, murderers; you name the crime, they committed it, and organized, which has always made it so tough to deal with foh us. Call themselves the Stoppagherra Society."

The Stoppagherra Society had been organized originally as a branch of the Mafia by four illegal immigrants who had been driven from Palermo by the Sicilian authorities and had arrived in New Orleans in 1869. With the help of hired assassins, they quickly eliminated all competition and soon became *the* single most powerful force dedicated to the rape and plunder of the city.

"They got richer and richer. They bought politicians, property, businesses, and badges. And what they couldn't buy, they just up and took. Robbery, extortion, murder—they stop at nothing," went on Montaigne. "Their favorite weapon is what we call the 'Mafia gun,' a shotgun with both barrels sawed off to about a foot and a half, and the stock sawed clean through neah the trigger and hollowed out."

He pulled open a drawer, bringing out just such a weapon wrapped in a soiled pillowcase. The stock had been fitted with hinges. One hand under the barrels, the other on top of the stock, he folded the weapon as easily as if it had been a jack-knife. He motioned Raider to stand.

"It fits inside youah coat on a hook, so . . ."

"What do they load it with?" asked Raider.

"Everything but catshit. Slugs, buckshot. Brother, theah's no weapon deadlier up to a hundred feet. None I evah seen."

The door opened. In came a tall, powerfully built man with a bristling black mustache, cold gray eyes, and hands that looked capable of doubling over the points of a drifting pick. Sergeant Montaigne greeted him, smiling.

"Dave, this is Mr. Weathahbee and Mr. Raidah, Pinkahton National Detective Agency. Fellows, meet Chief Hennessey."

Hennessey doffed his tall crown derby, placing it carefully on a coat hook and his mummie cloth worsted jacket on another. He dropped into the desk chair vacated by his associate and began rolling up his sleeves.

He was younger than Doc had pictured him. Chief Allan Pinkerton's words during their meeting in the Hotel Sunflower in Kansas City prior to their departure for New Orleans came back to him. David Hennessey was the son of a policeman who had been murdered in a coffeehouse shortly before David's twelfth birthday. A year after his father's death David became a messenger boy in the office of Chief of Police General A. S. Badger. In a few years he was appointed a detective. Aid, was what the locals called it, according to Pinkerton. He was teamed with his cousin, Mike Hennessey. Mike had been subsequently dismissed from the force for killing a corrupt superior who had tried to kill him. Mike drifted to Houston, where he opened his own private detective agency. Two years later he was murdered by an assassin said to have come from New Orleans expressly to kill him. Meanwhile, David, who had also been involved in the death of the corrupt captain, had, like Mike, been forced to give up his job. He too went to work for a private agency, rising to become superintendent, at which point he was reappointed to the police force by the newly elected reform mayor, Joseph Shakespeare.

From the day that he took the oath as Chief of Police, David Hennessey was marked for death by the Stoppagherra. Seven attempts had already been made on his life, the most recent involving a bomb placed in the tool box of his buggy, which fortunately had exploded before he'd gotten in, destroying the vehicle completely and sending one of the rear wheels forty feet through a half-inch plate-glass window.

"I been briefing the boys, Dave," said Montaigne.

Hennessey turned on an Irish grin that sent the coldness fleeing from his eyes and lit up the dim and dismal office.

"Heard enough yet to make you want to catch the first train out of here?" he asked.

"I been telling 'em how full we got ouh hands."

"All in a day's work," said Hennessey airily, at the same time glancing out the window. It had started to rain, a light, early spring shower, just enough to moisten the eaves troughs and set the streets shining.

"Days, nights." The chief fisted a yawn from his face. "I expect Frank told you this job's like shoveling hay into the wind, but one thing you can say, it's not dull."

"This recent rash of killings..." began Doc.

"Rash is right—eleven deaths in only ten days. We've had seventy unsolved murders in the past ten years, six more we did manage to connect with the culprits. Two executions, one twenty years in Parish Prison in Beauregard Square, and the other three let off with a tap on the rump. But, sad to say, we haven't been able to nail down a one of these latest. Our problem is Fat Tuesday."

Raider's and Doc's frowns brought explanation from the sergeant. "Mardi Gras," he explained. "This year Ash Wednesday comes early. Mardi Gras falls on the Tuesday before. Mardi Gras *is* New Orleans, the granddaddy of all our festivals. It's been our number-one institution since the city was founded."

"If this crime wave isn't stopped, and right away, it'll wreck Mardi Gras," added Hennessey. "Decent folks, even indecent'll be afraid to stick their heads out their doors, much less deck out in costumes, build floats, and everything else that goes with it. They'll probably cancel the Krewe of Twelfth Night Revelers ball. I realize all this doesn't sound like the end of the world to you boys, but to us natives it'd be a catastrophe. Like tearing the heart out of the woman you love. We'd be giving up to the mangy scum responsible, crawling down into our boots."

"It's making the fohce look helpless," said the sergeant in a grudging tone.

"Which is exactly what we are, Frank, let's face it." Hennessey sighed. "Boys"—he looked from one Pinkerton to the other—"that's the broad picture of what we're up against. Beginning this past January we've been working twelve- instead of eight-hour shifts, and we still can't keep up with the case load."

"The Sicilians are at the root o' everything," muttered Raider. "So says the sergeant."

"No question about that," said Hennessey. "Unfortunately, their connection to everything is indirect. They're very careful and clever about that. When they want somebody killed they always bring in an outside man. We've nailed a few, but it's impossible to tie them to the Stoppagherra. You know as well as I that before you go into court you've got to have all the belts tight on your case.

"Now, I want to be straight with you boys out front. It wasn't my idea to send for outside help, it was Mayor Shakespeare's. I'd frankly rather not have it, but he does, and he's the boss, so..." He shrugged. "But I'm not going to play games with you. I can't say I don't resent your being here. In my heart I do. But there comes a time when a man's got to be practical." He grinned. "Especially when his boss tells him to be. It's going to take time and a lot of legwork to get something solid on the Black Hand, the Stoppagherra, the Mafia, whatever you want to call it. We don't have the time or the manpower."

"We're so busy plugging up holes in the dike, we can't get around to diverting the rivah," said the sergeant.

Hennessey nodded. "That's about it. If you two can concentrate on just one aspect of this thing, breaking the Stoppagherra's—everybody calls it the Mafia's—hold on the waterfront, if you can line up even just a handful of their extortion victims who'd be willing to testify against them, it'd be like cutting the taproot on a tree. Everything up to the topmost leaves would wither and die. We want Esposito, Giuseppe Esposito, their number one."

Hennessey reached into a pigeonhole and brought out a blurred photograph of a ferret-faced man with a heavy black beard and mustache. His forehead was unusually low, and his bushy hair projected over it. He held the picture up for both of them, then handed it to Doc.

"Keep it," he said. "Fix that face in your minds."

He went on to describe Giuseppe Esposito as the most notorious and vicious Mafioso ever to set foot on American soil. He had arrived the previous March with rumors of a grisly tale swirling about his head. An English clergyman, the Reverend Mr. Rose, had been kidnapped by Esposito's boss, near Palermo. Ransom was sought from the minister's brother in England, and when the money failed to arrive, the gang cut off their prisoner's ears and sent them home. The British Parliament reacted swiftly, castigating the Italian government for its apparent indifference to the crime. Rome despatched troops to round up the gang. The leader was killed, but Esposito and six others escaped and were smuggled aboard a ship bound for the United States. They arrived in New York and eventually drifted to New Orleans.

"When Esposito got here, the head of the local Mafia was a man by the name of Tony Labruzzo. Three days after Esposito showed up, Labruzzo was shot down in Bienville Street. His body disappeared. It washed up in Barataria Bay two months later."

Doc gestured with the photograph. "How tall is he?"

"Only about five feet. I don't think he weighs a hundred pounds. He hangs around Jackson Square. He's got a house and keep rooms in various hotels."

"Let me get this straight," said Doc. "You're obviously convinced that the Mafia is behind the eleven murders." Both nodded. "So why do you want us to concentrate on the waterfront problem?"

"We're following up on the murders," said Hennessey. "As I said, if you can come up with people willing to testify against Esposito and his henchmen, District Attorney Luzenberg will be able to build a solid case against them. We can pack the ringleaders in a crate and ship them back to Sicily. Without the generals, the soldiers will scatter."

"If they succeed in forcing cancellation of the Mardi Gras they'll make every newspaper in the country," said Doc.

"That's what they want," said Montaigne. "Proof that they own the city."

"They own it already, of course," added Hennessey glumly. "They just have to prove they do on the outside. Can you think of a better way?"

Raider grunted. "You already tried to line up witnesses against this bunch, right?"

Hennessey and Montaigne both nodded, both reluctantly.

"What makes you think we're gonna have any better luck?"

"To be honest, I don't," said Hennessey. "I'm hoping you can be more persuasive, more convincing. One of our problems is we've got Italians on the force. The situation's reached a point where one Italian doesn't trust another, even his best friend, in uniform or out. We obviously can't fire our Italian officers. Oh, we've weeded out a few bad apples, but the vast majority are honest, hardworking boys."

"Folks don't generally open up to strangers," said Raider.

"Take it easy, Rade," said Doc. "Let's at least give it a whirl before you dump on it."

"Who's dumping? Not me."

Doc laughed. "As you two may have noticed, my partner's not the most optimistic soul."

Raider glared, but made no comment.

"All I ask," said Hennessey, "is that one of you check in every so often. Give us a progress report. We won't be breathing down your necks, it's just that we might be able to help. You know, add something, maybe give you a tip that'll prevent a wild goose chase or warn you off somebody we know who's a waste of time to chin with."

Doc nodded. "We'll check in. Does this Esposito use any aliases?"

"None we know of. Man's brazen as they come. He carries a nine-inch stiletto and knows how to use it, so if your paths cross, watch yourselves. And he's rarely alone. I'll be honest with you—he's got the legitimate merchants on the waterfront shaking in their shoes. All we can hope for is that you'll come across a few more angry, more bitter than they are afraid."

Doc got to his feet. "We'll do our best, Chief. About the killings—is any pattern showing up?"

"All knifings. All the bodies found in alleys near cathouses. We've questioned the nearest madams and girls in each instance, but of course they're deaf, dumb, and blind."

They shook hands all around. Raider and Doc started for the door, preceded by the two officers. In the corridor Hennessey spoke again.

"One thing more, boys." He stopped, lowering his head as a uniformed policeman rounded the corner and came toward them. Clearing his throat, the chief nodded the man past them. He went out the front door. Hennessey glanced up and down the corridor. "Nobody in town outside of Frank here, the mayor, and me has to know you're working with us. You can pose as anything you please—anything but the law. You can be two preachers, for all I care. It's up to you. Make friends, try and get into folks' confidences, follow me? When you do, if you can, then pin them down."

"Understood," said Doc.

"Where are you staying?"

"Hotel Gregg."

The chief clucked lightly, shook his head, and grinned. "One of the few respectable hotels in town. Oh well, you're not going to have much time for socializing anyway."

All four stood outside the double doors. The rain was still coming down, slightly harder, stringing crystal beads along the edge of the overhang, stretching, plopping onto the bricks and forming puddles in the glistening street. Raider pulled his collar up and tipped his Stetson slightly toward the back of his head to catch the downpour on the front of the brim, sluice it around the sides, and drop it off the back, clear off his jacket.

"One last question," said Doc to Hennessey. "How many in Esposito's gang?"

Hennessey questioned Montaigne with his eyes. The sergeant shrugged.

"About three hundred."

Doc whistled softly. "That's a lot of muscle. Three hundred bodyguards for Mr. Hair."

"Yeah," said Raider morosely. "On top o' his nine-inch pig sticker."

They said good night. Few hansoms were visible in the street, and those they saw were in use. It was a seven-block walk to the hotel, and every soggy, squishy step added fuel to Raider's pessimism; every block added another complaint to their lot. His remarks, delivered in his customary whine and liberally laced with expletives, was rapidly assuming the length of a boardinghouse laundry list.

"I don't like this place, Doc. I don't like cities, period. They make me uncomfortable as hell. I never had to work on a case in a city afore."

"What about Kansas City? That Wells Fargo case two years ago."

"That was in an' out, mostly out."

"San Francisco, four years back."

"That was a cuppa coffee an' back in the saddle. Jesus Christ, man can't even ride a damn horse here. Everybody rides round in buggies an' hansoms, except you can't get either when the rain comes down. An' we're stuck here like two hogs in a well, you know. That Sicilian son of a bitch . . ."

"Esposito."

"He's sure not gonna pack up an' run. He an' his three hundred pals an' his nine-inch bone pick got a home here. They're sticking. This is their home turf. How we supposed to find the bastard? Oh, find him, sure, but I mean get the goods on him. We never had us anything like this afore, nothing close. Bank robbers, Wells Fargo, railroad turnovers, killing, sure, but respectable . . ." Doc laughed. "You know what I mean, not sneaking round whorehouse back alleys. This is undercover, an' you know me an' undercover, I stink at it. I like working out in the open, shove them down behind one rock and us behind another an' let fly." He glanced about warily, worriedly. "I don't like this town, it's strange."

"Nothing strange about it. It's just a trifle crime-ridden, that's all."

"I like what you call 'a trifle.' This here's hell's headquarters, you bet you."

His hand went to his Peacemaker, as if to assure him that it was still fattening its holster.

"That's another thing," he plainted peevishly. "These bastards don't know decent weapons. All they know is knives an' razors an' poison in your whiskey. Know something? What I really hate 'bout cities is they're so damn close, all the buildings crowd each other so, sunlight can't get between the cracks. Some sunlight! I bet all it ever does down here is rain. You know something else? That hotel room stinks."

"That's furniture wax, Rade. Every respectable hotel offers

clean rooms. Clean rooms include clean washbasins and polished furniture. You're so used to vomit and stale whiskey,
cheap whorefume and mildew you don't recognize a halfway
decent odor when you smell it."

"Horseshit!" They walked in silence, then: "Doc?"

"What now?"

"How long you think this shindig is gonna take us? How
long afore we can pack up and get out?"

"Why don't you ask me how long before the Mississippi
changes direction? How the devil would I know? You heard
the man—we know who we've got to nail, who we've got to
talk to, where we find them. What could be simpler? We've
never had it so easy."

"You're funny as hell."

"One of us should try to be. You're about as pleasant as
the weather."

On they strolled in silence. Near silence. Two steps behind
his partner Raider continued mumbling to himself, and every
so often casting about anxiously. A whore in a doorway focused
her painted smile upon him out from under her umbrella.

"Hi, big boy."

"Hi and go to hell."

"You go to hell!"

"Go home an' tell your maw to be 'shamed o' you, damn
bedwhacker!"

"Fag!"

"Whore!"

"Rade . . ."

They walked on, the lady's raunchy resentment ringing in
Raider's reddening ears.

"Bitch whore."

They came within sight of the Hotel Gregg.

"One thing we've got working for us, Rade—anonymity."

"I s'pose. The main thing is nobody round here knows us.
Hennessey's right, we oughta have us a cover. Maybe we could
pose as a couple drummers."

"How about two real-estate brokers from up-country? That
way if anybody's curious we won't have to show any wares,
just fake it."

"Maybe."

They wandered through the lobby. The desk clerk nodded,

smiling. The lobby smelled damp; the potted palms drooped dejectedly. The rain, rising in intensity, thrashed the windows. A man displaying a watch chain three-quarters of an inch wide over his ample belly sat with his face in the *True Delta*. The front-page right-hand corner headline announced discovery of the eleventh corpse in ten days.

Doc secured their key and together they mounted the carpeted stairs, making their way down the corridor to room 2E. Inside they noted that the maid had tidied up in their absence, both beds made and turned down. On the pillow of the one to the right was a piece of paper.

Doc gasped; Raider swallowed. On the paper lay a freshly severed human hand. It had been dipped in tar, the odor distinctly recognizable.

Moving to the bed, Raider jerked the paper out from under it. There was a note scrawled in red letters: *"Welcome to New Orleans, Pinks."*

CHAPTER TWO

"Dump it in the wastebasket, Rade."

"You . . ."

Doc moved toward the bed. Evident distaste masking his handsome face, he was preparing to pick up the severed hand when Raider spoke, freezing him where he stood.

"Wait, don't throw it away. We'll keep it."

Doc stared in disbelief. "What?"

"Keep it and return it to the bastards. Track down where Mr. Hair sleeps and lay it on *his* damn pillow."

"Don't be ridiculous. We don't have time to play games."

"It's no game, it's not getting even, it's letting him know we don't scare."

"Speak for yourself. Be sensible. What are you going to do, fold it up into a fist and carry it around in your pocket?"

"Hell no. Wrap it up in, in . . ." He undid his bandana from around his neck. "Give it here."

"Take it."

Raider muttered disparagingly, shouldered Doc gently to

one side, and wrapped the hand up as if it were a sandwich. Then he placed it on the closet shelf.

"In two days it's going to start stinking to high heaven," said Doc.

"In two days it'll be back where it come from."

"You realize this changes the whole picture." Doc sighed long and mournfully. "What luck! We haven't been here two hours and already our cover's shot full of holes. What am I saying? We hadn't even decided on a cover."

"We did too."

"Rade, Rade, Rade, they know we're here. They've got eyes all over the place."

"So what."

They discussed the unfortunate turn and its possible consequences, deciding that it would be best to split up, work the waterfront independently.

"We'll meet every night at ten," ventured Doc, warming to his ideas as they poured forth. "A different spot each night. We'll have to get identical maps, and every night when we meet to compare notes we'll decide on where we'll be meeting the next night. And I think, under the circumstances, we should seriously consider disguises."

"Oh, fuck that shit! Goddamn beards and specs and funny hats? Hair on my face that doesn't grow out of it natural always itches like fury. In this heat I'll be scratching myself raw. Please, Doc, no disguises. I can't stand that spirit gum. I can never get it to stick where it's supposed to and keep it from sticking where it shouldn't."

"All right, all right, all right. We'll play it straight." Doc glanced at the open closet and the neatly wrapped hand reposing on the shelf. "You could get your head blown off, trying to put that thing back. Is it really worth it?"

"It is to me, damn it!"

"Why not find out where Esposito lives and mail it to him?"

"On accounta I don't operate like that. You think I'm 'fraid o' the bastard?"

Doc yawned, stretched, and removed his jacket. "Let's get some sleep. You know, you could ask the desk clerk how it got here. You could question the maid."

"Screw that. It's not important; getting it back to him is." He shuddered.

"What are you shuddering for?"

"I'm not."

"You just did, I saw you."

"You're fulla crap!"

"How are you going to sleep with that thing on the shelf? What if it comes after you in the middle of the night, gets loose, drops off the shelf, pulls itself across the floor, up the leg of the bed, down the covers, up to your throat..."

"Oh, shut up!"

The severed hand did not attack Raider during the night, but his concern that it might managed to keep him awake until shortly before dawn. He was bleary-eyed and irritable at breakfast, seemingly envious of his partner's well-rested appearance.

"I slept like the proverbial log," said Doc.

"I know, you keep saying. That's great, beautiful. Who gives a shit?"

"Keep your voice down, Rade, the waitress'll hear you."

The waitress approached them, pad in hand, a pencil stuck in her hair. Raider gasped. Doc winced and covered his face with his hand to keep from bursting out laughing. It was the umbrella lady from the doorway with whom Raider had had passing words the previous night. She recognized him instantly.

"What do you want?" she snarled.

"Eggs over lightly, ham, and light toast," said Doc.

"Same," said Raider uncomfortably, avoiding her eyes, "only heavy both."

She scribbled, muttered, glared, and departed.

"Jesus Christ," growled Raider. "She'll probably pour arsenic in my goddamn yolks." He glanced about the dining room. The place was about half filled. The clicking of silver, the soft sound of liquids pouring into cups and glasses blended with low, indistinguishable conversations. "This sure isn't the most popular beanery in town. No wonder she got to work nights."

"Supplemental income, Rade. She's probably putting herself through college."

Long before the Pinkertons arrived in the Crescent City, two rival factions of the New Orleans Mafia had gone to war over a most coveted and valuable prize—control of the city's piers and the unloading of bananas from Honduras. The center of the city became a battleground when the two sides clashed at Clairborne and Esplanade streets. Gang members of both factions were wounded and killed, and flying bullets hit pedestrians. But, despite the public outrage over the incident, nothing was done to curb the growing ambition of Giuseppe Esposito, the victors' leader. Mr. Hair's trusted friends and first lieutenants were the Matranga brothers, Charles and Tony. So fond of Tony was Esposito that he placed him in command of the Supreme Council of Twenty, which prepared the extortion letters, planned the murders, assigned the assassins, and generally orchestrated and controlled crime in the city. For his part, Esposito was content to play the role of overlord—a godfather figure to the mob—sit back, and collect hundreds of thousands of dollars from the immense profits of the organization's various illicit enterprises.

For many years, long before Esposito arrived from Sicily, George, Joe, and Peter Provenzano had enjoyed a monopoly: unloading the fruit ships from South and Central America and distributing the produce. They held legal contracts with the various shipping companies and employed several hundred laborers. The men were paid forty cents an hour for day work, sixty cents at night—fair wages. The Provenzanos became rich and politically influential. They were honest; their only connection with the Mafia was in the fulfillment of two basic requirements necessary for the continuation of their business: They paid tribute to the society regularly; they employed men sent to them by the Matrangas. These employees, though relatively few in number, provided the Matrangas with a built-in espionage network which effectively kept the Provenzanos in line and assured the continued payment of monthly "contributions."

On one occasion only did the Provenzanos take steps to break the mob's stranglehold on their lucrative business. Approached by Chief Hennessey, Peter Provenzano heard him out, accepted his offer of protection, and agreed to testify against the Matranga brothers and Giuseppe Esposito in court. Peter was the youngest of the three brothers. His patience had become exhausted. He was prepared to risk his life to destroy the mob.

He never reached court. Two days after his secret meeting

with Hennessey, Peter Provenzano was found in a flour barrel in his office, bound and gagged. He had been tied in such a manner—with his legs drawn tightly up to his stomach—that, when in agony, he had tried to straighten them, he strangled himself.

It was under these circumstances and with this knowledge in mind that Doc approached George and Joe Provenzano at ten o'clock in the morning in their office following an earlier briefing with Sergeant Montaigne at headquarters. George was the bigger of the two brothers, bigger and tougher-looking than David Hennessey, reflected Doc as he introduced himself, offering his hand and losing it entirely in the mitt-like grasp of the other. So big and bulky was George that when he sat in his chair it all but vanished beneath him, creaking plaintively and threatening to shatter. He affected a full beard, mustache, and sideburns. Brother Joe, meanwhile, leaned against a desk, his muscular arms folded, a suspicious look on his mustachioed face. Doc was a stranger, *felt* like a stranger. His two hosts were definitely on their guard, he decided. Getting either to open up to him, much less their promise to follow their dead younger brother's lead and agree to testify in court, would be a miracle on a par with Creation itself.

"You say you're in real estate, Mr. . . . ."

"Hastings. That's correct. Down from New Iberia. No sense beating about the bush. You two gentlemen control the waterfront, actually own a sizable chunk of the land, the piers, equipment . . ."

"We're not interested in selling," said George.

"I'm sure you're not. Who would be, eh? Mind if I smoke?"

They exchanged glances. Joe shook his head in approval. Doc brought out two Old Virginia cheroots, offering them. They declined wordlessly. Pocketing one, he lit the other, using a stove match on the sole of his shoe. He hadn't the foggiest idea of how to proceed, he realized, how to open the wound. Which described it aptly. However he attempted to do so he could easily picture shaking heads, scowls, movement, and a polite but firm request that he leave. He puffed, his mind racing.

"Just what is it you want, Mr. Hastings?" asked Joe. "We're not selling anything. Not buying, either."

Doc took a deep breath and jumped: straight into the lion's mouth. He could almost hear the jaws clacking shut behind and feel the moist, foul-smelling darkness all around him.

"How would you two like to get rid of your silent partners? Permanently?"

"What partners?" Joe asked, his eyes narrowing and brightening menacingly.

George frowned. "We got no partners."

"I'm talking about the Matrangas, Giuseppe Esposito, and the rest of the scum."

George rose from his chair, swung open the door, and stepped aside. Outside, the sun glared ferociously, bouncing off the dark, debris-littered water gently lapping at the pilings. Seagulls *gah-gah-gahed,* and a lone pelican, perched on a piling, repositioned its ridiculous-looking feet and stared down its hook-tipped bill at Doc.

"Out," snapped George. "And keep walking, fast and far. If you know what's good for you."

Doc puffed and made no move to get up. "It's what's good for you two that concerns me."

"Who the hell are you?" blurted Joe nervously, releasing the edge of the desk and suddenly towering over Doc.

"Hastings. U.S. Secret Service. The government's taking over, boys. We're going to wipe out the Mafia, starting right here. I mean *here,* on the docks." He glanced from one to the other, hardening his eyes. "With your cooperation. Or without it."

Without another word, he got up, rescued his curl-brimmed derby from the desktop, flicked the ashes from his cheroot into the spittoon, and started out. George shut the door in his face before he could set foot over the sill.

"U. S. Secret Service?"

"George, for chrissakes..."

"Take it easy, Joe, I'll handle this. Prove it, mister. Let's see your badge or license, whatever the hell you people carry." Holding forth his shovel-sized hand, he snapped his fingers.

"Are you crazy? You think I carry legitimate I.D. on me? A badge, for your information—you think I'd carry mine in this burg? Down here, with half the Mafia unloading your bananas? All I'd have to do is run into the wrong fist, get kayoed, frisked, and my badge found. Good-bye me, good-bye operation. Right out the window. Use your heads. Do I look like a Mafioso to you? A spy?" Slowly they shook their heads. "Do you think I'd come down here and stick my neck out three feet if I wasn't on the up and up? Come on, do you? Hold it, don't answer right away, think it over."

He talked and talked, painting lurid word pictures of the government's impending involvement, the reasons for it, the growing public demand that the Mafia be completely eradicated once and for all. George listened; Joe listened. When Doc was done, when his last argument had been voiced and considered by both his listeners, Joe shook his head slowly.

"We can't help you," he said quietly.

"We don't know what you're talking about, Mafia people working for us. We don't know any Mafia."

"How about Peter, did he know any?"

"Let's not get into that," said Joe tightly, his voice suddenly sad. "He's no business of yours."

"Is he yours? He *was* your brother. Don't you owe him something?"

"He played it stupid," said Joe. "He was either drunk or crazy. We didn't know anything about it. It was all his idea."

"I'm sure it was. But whether it was or wasn't isn't the point. The important thing is he was willing to cooperate. He got up the courage..."

"Look what it got him," said George dryly.

Joe nodded. "Forget it, mister. We don't want anything to do with Hennessey, the mayor, you, the government, nobody. Just leave us alone and let us run our business."

"Okay, if that's the way you want it. But I'll tell you something: We're going to get them. Every one. Right down to the twelve-year-olds running their errands. Them and everybody who does business with them. With any connection whatsoever, no matter how remote. You want to keep on running your business? Good luck. But you may find it a little hard to run from behind bars."

"We're clean," snapped George menacingly. "We don't break any laws."

"Then you've got nothing to worry about. Good day gentlemen."

Doc strode to the door, jerked it wide, and went out. The pelican flew off with a sound like canvas flapping. His hand on the knob, Doc turned.

"See you in court."
He slammed the door.

PELICAN BOOK SHOP
Books New and Used

Raider walked leisurely by the shop on his way to Jackson Square in the French Quarter. He had parted company with Doc after breakfast, wishing his partner well on Doc's visit to the waterfront. Reluctant to duplicate the well-dressed one's efforts, Raider decided to plan his own day around locating Giuseppe Esposito and tailing him in the hope of getting to know the Mafia leader's habits, meeting places, and general activities.

He felt acutely conspicuous in his Stetson, denim jacket and trousers, and hand-tooled calfskin Middleton boots, with his six-gun at his hip. Everyone's eyes were on him as he sauntered into the square. Doc had warned him, he recalled, advising him to better protect himself by "dressing city." Raider had ignored his counsel. The Mafia knew they had come to town; the severed hand on the pillow confirmed it. They had to know as well what both looked like. They had eyes everywhere. What good would it do to exchange his Stetson for a fedora?

The severed hand. . . . He stopped so short he nearly fell forward, his hat tilting to the front. Snapping his fingers, he spun about, retracing his steps to the Pelican Book Shop. The sun broiled the street. Ladies passing by fanned themselves delicately with their hankies; men sweated; cats slept in doorways; dogs crept into the shade and lay motionless. If it was this hot at nine-fifteen in the morning, he thought ruefully, what would it be like at high noon?

"Hell turned upside down."

Long, narrow tables piled with used books, many in disreputable condition, stretched away from either side of the door. More books were stacked in the windows. Inside, seemingly every available inch save the space occupied by the cash register held books, books, books. Customers browsed: women with parasols depending from their wrists, two wide-eyed schoolboys examining a slender volume of Elizabeth Barrett Browning's poetry. The old lady behind the counter looked like a frigate under full sail, her leg-o'-mutton sleeves puffed out, her monstrous breastworks riding high and so nearly level that she could easily have served breakfast to her man without a tray. Her hair looked like sloppily coiled steel wool and framed a face with an expression so sour it could have stopped a bull in its tracks, mused Raider.

He moved slowly up a narrow aisle between two tables piled high with volumes. Each table displayed a hand-lettered sign stuck in the center like a flag on a rampart: "ANY BOOK 50 CENTS." He poked through a pile and located the biggest one he could find. He hefted it, judging it at close to five pounds, a foot tall on edge, and a good four inches thick. He grinned at the title: *The Fate of Mankind,* by Wallace Depew Horton, Ph.D. At the counter he paid his fifty cents and asked to have it wrapped.

"We don't wrap 'em, mister. It's cash and carry for used."

"Can't you make believe it's new? Do me a favor, can't you? Wrap it in pretty paper."

"Cost you a nickel."

Raider's face sagged. "Oh . . ." He thought a moment. "How 'bout you give me the paper and string and I wrap it myself. For two cents."

"Do you want the book or not?"

"Okay, okay."

She wrapped *The Fate of Mankind* in blue paper, secured it with bag string, and shoved it at him. Tucking it under his arm, he was on his way out the door when a pretty young girl under an enormous and outrageous hat—a flowered, beribboned resting place for a stuffed bird—came careening into him, knocking his purchase from under his arm and his hat from his head.

"Mercy me, I'm so sorry! Do fohgive me."

She bent low, dropping her tightly slung, large, and attractive charms before his widening eyes. She retrieved his book and his hat, straightened, and handed them to him with a schoolgirl curtsy.

"'Scuse me," he mumbled.

"Oh, no, no, no. It was all mah doing. Ah wasn't looking, silly me. Just came barreling in . . ."

She was pretty, with big cornflower blue eyes, a complexion as flawless and fresh-looking as a child's, full lips with a pert little nose, pink roses in her cheeks. Abruptly, she stopped speaking and stared at him.

"Say that again."

"What? 'Scuse me?"

She pointed to his hat. "You Oklahoma? Texas?"

"Arkansas, back when."

"Is that a fact? Mercy!"

"You a razorback?"

"No, ah'm originally from Tulsa, but mah best friend's from Arkansas. Fulton County."

"You're kidding! I'm from Fulton County, near Viola."

"Dulcie Mae's from Salem."

"County seat. Small world."

"Oh my but she'd love to meet you, Mr. . . . ."

"O'Toole. John O'Toole." Raider touched his hat brim.

"John O'Toole, John B. Stetson, six-gun, horse boots, and all, my, my! Hey, what y'all doing now, John O'Toole?"

"Heading back to the hotel."

"Where y'all staying?"

"Over on St. Charles."

"Y'all wait here, I'll go fetch Dulcie Mae. Oh, but she's going to do handstands when I tell her I bumped into somebody from little old Fulton County. She'll raise the flag!" She started off.

"Wait, wait!"

"Billy. Billy Cobb." Turning back, she offered her hand. He shook it.

"Billy, I got things to do right now." Disappointment shadowed her smile, coming down over it like a window shade being drawn. "Maybe later on today, okay?"

Back came her smile. "This aftahnoon? This aftahnoon. At the Bird Cage." Again she swung about, pointing across the street. "Ovah yonder. See the yellow sign? We'll be waiting. Y'all will come, won't you? Dulcie Mae'll be dying to meet y'all." She paused and appraised him. "My, but you're a tall one. How tall are y'all?"

"Ten foot two."

She giggled and slapped him on the arm, nearly knocking the book loose. And they were friends.

He hurried back to the Hotel Gregg, confused, uncertain as to exactly how he had fallen into Billy Cobb's clutches. Not

exactly her clutches, but met her and come to know her practically intimately on such short notice. She was a working girl,
he could always tell. Not necessarily by how they looked. She
didn't have to be filling a doorway or standing under a street
lamp. It wasn't even the clothes. It was in the eyes. Come
hither, Doc called it, invitation to drop and flop. A promise of
fun and a demand for payment squeezed together as clear as a
bell ringing, blue eyes, green eyes, brown, always the gleam,
always the same. Of course, some were brazener than their
sisters, some foul-mouthed as a riverman, and some up front
so with their goodies they'd make you want to turn around and
walk off. But others, like Billy Cobb, were ladies; at least they
tried to act so: not loud, no flasharity, not wetting their lips
with the tip of their tongue, no little suggestive rearranging of
their posture.

Only the telltale gleam.

He stopped at the front desk. The clerk looked up from his
Times-Democrat. It crossed Raider's mind that the man hadn't
been out of doors with the sun out in six years, so pasty-faced
was he. Pockmarks scarred both cheeks, and a nick where he'd
cut himself shaving, and his lower lip drooped on the right, as
if buried deep in it was a lead sinker. He stared out of his pink
and watery eyes.

"You got a pen and red ink I could borrow?" asked Raider.

"Got a pen. No red ink."

"Got anything red?"

The clerk sighed impatiently, put down his paper, and began
going through drawers. Each held more junk, odds and ends,
than the one before. He found a red crayon, holding it up.

"That'll do fine. I'll bring it back."

Upstairs in the privacy of 2E, he unwrapped *The Fate of
Mankind*, got out his razor, and laboriously began cutting a
large rectangular opening in the pages, slicing through twenty
or more at a time, taking care to avoid cutting through to the
edge. When he was done, he inserted the contents of the bandana. To his elation, it fit perfectly. Picking up the crayon, he
wrote inside the cover.

"Delited to be here."

Doc came away from his visit with the Provenzano brothers
understandably disappointed, but on second thought he ac-

knowledged that he hadn't hoped for any smashing success, considering the situation. What he had accomplished was simply to introduce himself to George and Joe, lay the cards on the table, and leave them with something to think about.

Would they think? Would they discuss it? Would they change their minds? Hardly. He'd be amazed if they did, though that wouldn't prevent him from checking back with them either later in the day or first thing tomorrow.

If only one or the other harbored a tiny spark of vengeance, a latent desire, however small, to get even with the Matrangas for murdering Peter. A desire strong enough to overcome their fear of losing their lives as painfully and ignominiously as had he.

What next? He would talk to the dock workers. Not a pleasant prospect, nor one that promised to be productive. To begin with, how could he possibly tell the difference between the Provenzanos' people and the Matrangas' spies? Two words to the wrong man and he might not even get back to the hotel with his blood supply intact!

No. He'd have to examine the situation in considerably more depth before buttonholing any of the workers. Search out all his options, plan his every move from now on carefully and intelligently. Nothing impulsive, no hunches, only the best possible stragegy. Should he get together with Hennessey and Montaigne again? Perhaps.

The two surviving Provenzanos were the key, the more he thought about it, turning his steps toward the center of the city. He hadn't exactly struck out with them. He hadn't been thrown out with a string of threats ringing in his ears and the door slamming. Actually, he'd been the one who'd slammed the door.

Hennessey was the big problem. He had given his ironclad promise to Peter that he would protect him, and had failed to. Which meant that in George's and Joe's eyes the chief and the police force were not to be trusted. The mob was everywhere—all-seeing, all-knowing. Anybody who trusted anybody else in this town had to be either naïve or a fool. He chuckled grimly to himself, wondering in passing if George and Joe trusted each other.

What was Raider up to? he wondered. He planned to track down Esposito and tail him. They had argued over it briefly

before parting earlier. How can you shadow anybody, standing
out like the proverbial sore thumb, sporting a ten-gallon hat in
a sea of derbies and fedoras? You might as well carry a flag.
Still, there had been no talking him out of his beloved John
B. Divesting him of it would be something like taking away
his navel, or some other portion of his anatomy.

The whole situation was so damned complicated, and getting
more so by the minute.

"Ah me, when are we ever going to get an easy case dumped
in our laps? Will either of us ever live to see such an unlikely
eventuality? Will we?"

His question drew an immediate response, in the nature of
a somewhat contrary comment. A gull, straying from the waterfront and soaring overhead, squawked impudently and let fly,
depositing a blob of intestinal residue, wetly and accurately
dead center on the crown of Doc's derby.

Raider hung around Jackson Square, his gift for his quarry
tucked under one arm, until three in the afternoon, his stomach
juices gurgling in impatient appeal for nourishment. But he
refused to take time out for lunch. Nor did he venture near the
Bird Cage. The bell of St. Louis Cathedral, located across from
the Chartres Street entrance to Jackson Square, tolled the hour
just as a hansom pulled up before the hotel directly opposite
him. A moment later off it rolled, revealing its passenger standing there surveying the square.

Giuseppe Esposito. No mistaking the diminutive hairy one.
He was hatless. Raider had never seen so much hair on a human
before. It rivaled a monkey's in abundance. He appeared swar-
thier than his photograph, and, since he was standing barely
fifty feet from him, Raider could clearly see the scars on his
cheeks and forehead. He looked as if somebody had worked
him over with a penknife.

Glancing up and down the way, the little man retreated
inside the hotel. Raider gave him a full minute before starting
across the street and ascending the front steps into the lobby.
He entered just in time to see Esposito vanish up the stairs. He
started boldly up after him. The desk clerk called to him.

"Suh, suh! Wheah are you goin'?"

"Up to see my horse," replied Raider blandly. The clerk
scowled and started to protest, but just then an elderly, white-

maned man in a frock coat two sizes too large for him stepped up to the desk and hammered the bell, commanding the clerk's attention.

Raider paused at the top of the stairs, looking left and right. No sign of Esposito, but he could hear steps softly ascending to the next floor. He followed. The little man's room was at the end of the third-floor hallway, just beyond a large and ugly sand-filled ash receiver. He had gotten out his key and was preparing to unlock the door when he looked up and saw Raider. His expression questioned. Raider hurried forward.

"Mr. Esposito?"

"Who you?" he asked in a thick accent.

"Present for you . . ."

He proffered the book. Esposito stiffened, snarled, batted the book to the floor, and shrank into the corner like a snake poising to strike. His hand shot under his jacket; out came a pistol. But Raider was too fast, whipping and leveling his Peacemaker. The cannon in Esposito's hand tilted, and his face fell into his chin.

"Drop it and open the door."

The gun tumbled to the carpet. Raider closed on him menacingly.

"You gonna kill me?"

He was shaking as if an electric current was pulsing through his scrawny body, his knees bending slightly and tapping together.

"Open it or I'll blow you through it." He did so, nodding so hard his head threatened to snap from his neck. "Now, pick up your present and get inside."

He turned to retrieve the book, and hesitated. "Is a *bomba . . . ?*"

"Pick it up!"

He did so and backed inside. Raider kicked the gun on the floor into the room, snatching it up, jamming it into his belt. He heeled the door shut behind him. The room was small—a corner with two windows overlooking the street and a third overlooking a narrow alley filled with the squabbling of cats. At Raider's order, Esposito, his hands trembling, opened the wrapping. And the book.

"Put it on the bed. Now, show me your friend."

"Friend?"

"That pig sticker you carry around. The knife, stupid! Get it out, pronto!"

"Si, si."

He produced the stiletto from an inside pocket.

"Open it."

With a swift jerking motion of his wrist, he deftly flicked it open. It was gleaming, deadly.

"Good. Now, pick up the hand and cut off the thumb. You're gonna eat it. I'm gonna watch."

"Madre di Dio . . ."

"You don't like thumbs? How 'bout a finger?"

"You crazy."

"Listen to me, you little piece o' shit, two-legged garbage. I could blow you into the street. Don't think I wouldn't love to." He could feel tingling in his finger as he tightened on the trigger. "Purely. But I'm not going to, not now. But one night real soon I'm gonna come back. I'm gonna come in while you're sleeping, snoring away like a baby. I'm gonna stick this in your eye and blow your goddamn brains through your pillow, you understand?"

"Si, si."

"Si, si, your asshole!"

Muttering, he pushed him down on the bed with the gun and departed with a promise:

"You so much as show your ugly face at the goddamn window. I'll kill you from down in the street, understand?"

He got out. Hurrying down the stairs, he rushed across the lobby, bounded down the front steps, nearly losing the cannon from his belt as he did so. He paused briefly on the sidewalk, getting his bearings, and then set out in the direction of the Bird Cage. Halfway across the square, passing through the shadow of General Stonewall Jackson astride his rearing horse, his hat raised in salute, Raider stopped.

As he did so he felt eyes on him. He turned. Esposito was standing at the window, his hand raised, his finger pointing. At him. A rifle cracked. The shot came from St. Louis Cathedral at the distant end of the square. He ducked behind a huge clump of azaleas. A second shot whistled through the blossoms, ringing off the iron fence, coming so close it practically shaved his chin. He flattened and got out his six-gun.

There were two of them, standing just inside the open church door. He fired and cursed. What the hell am I doing, he thought, shooting at a church! Women screamed and ran; men fled for cover. In seconds the entire square was emptied. It was crazy, he thought, a shoot-out smack in the middle of town, broad daylight, two of Esposito's choirboy bodyguards out to make points with the hairy one.

Quicky, expertly, they bracketed the bush; it was suddenly too hot, too porous for cover. Bunching his body, he sprang to the right, drawing three quick shots, hitting the ground at the base of the statue under the words THE UNION MUST BE, SHALL BE PRESERVED. Screw the Union, he thought, never mind the ten tons of statue, preserve this old boy! He kneed and elbowed his way around to the far side. He got off two shots, drawing four quick responses, kicking dirt in his face. They were good, he thought; they could pin him down there until they got reinforcements to come up on him from the opposite end, pinching him between. Again he fired, the blast echoing across the open area. He threw a look. His heart jumped. One of them suddenly got careless and showed his face. Raider fired. The slug smashed off the side of the door, ricocheting squarely into the careless one's face, jerking his head back, all but snapping it free of his neck. He screamed, dropped his rifle, and covered up. Down on his knees he fell and over on his face. His companion quit cold, turned, and started dragging him back into the shadows.

Raider slowly got to his feet, crouched, and dashed to the cover of the nearest well-shadowed doorway. He glanced up at the hotel window. Esposito was gone. Amazing, he thought. No cops, no casualties, thank God; except for the bodyguard, no nothing, save for a bruise on his left knee and a lingering case of the shakes.

"Damn place is wider open than Silver City on Saturday night!"

He reloaded and took up his vigil. Billy Cobb and Dulcie Mae Whatever could wait.

The church bells sounded the quarter hour and the hands of the clock in the drugstore window next door took up the task of monitoring his time. He glanced about the square. To the north and south he could see the Pontalba buildings occupying the entire block on St. Peter and St. Ann streets. Interwoven in the ironwork in hundreds of places was the monogram of Almonaster-Pontalba.

Few people were about. Little wonder: The heat was ferocious. Just crossing the square had worked him up into an awesome sweat. He was soaked to the skin. Was it the sun, he wondered, or nerves? He saw himself back in the narrow hallway, saw again Esposito going for his gun, and himself beating him to the draw. It hadn't been the smartest play he'd ever made—he smiled to himself—but damned if it wasn't satisfying. At least the slimy bastard now knew they were playing for keeps.

As if him and his bunch weren't!

At twenty-two past Esposito appeared, as calm and self-possessed as a deacon. He had changed into a gray suit and fedora and was carrying a walking stick. Raider watched him set sail down the street.

"Mr. O'Toole, Mr. O'Toole!"

Billy Cobb in all her available glory came running up, preceding a lovely with lime-green eyes. She was poured into a flouncy-hemmed and cuffed and bibbed red and black dress that couldn't have been more complimentary to her curves. One look and Raider had to catch himself to keep from whistling aloud. At the same time he could feel a slight but recognizable tingling in his manhood. Billy grabbed his arm.

"Wheah you been? We been looking all ovah. This is—"

"'Scuse me, ladies, I don't like to be rude, but I can't stop. I got urgent business."

Freeing his arm, he looked away from her smile to Esposito, his hand on his hat to keep the breeze from stealing it, picking up the pace, heading for the corner. In another five seconds he would be out of sight.

"What business?" asked Billy. She followed his eyes. "With him, Mr. E.?"

"You know him?"

"Not like Dulcie Mae I don't."

She tittered into one lace-gloved hand and turned to Dulcie Mae, who had come up behind her. Dulcie Mae colored slightly. Raider's quarry, meantime, had vanished, but the Pinkerton paid no heed. His interest in Billy's companion was suddenly aroused.

"You know him?" he asked.

"You bet she does." Again Billy laughed. The obvious jumped up in front of Raider, grabbing him by the throat. Dulcie Mae *knew* Mr. Hair in the Biblical sense, he concluded. Which had to mean a good deal more about him than he wanted her to know. He grinned inwardly. Who doesn't talk too much in bed?

"How 'bout I buy you two pretty ladies a drink? What do you say?"

Billy looped her arm through his. "What do y'all think we say?"

All three started toward the Bird Cage. Raider stopped at the corner.

"Tell me something," he said. "Either o' you know how to spell the word delighted?"

"Sure," said Billy. "D-e-l-i-t-e-d, delighted."

Raider beamed. "I thought so."

CHAPTER THREE

Doc lunched alone in the Pontchartrain Hotel dining room on St. Charles Avenue, taking advantage of Raider's absence. It wasn't his partner's type of place. He would have felt as uncomfortable as a bird in a cage full of toms, as he himself had once described his feelings at a church wedding. A string trio played Mozart, and the other diners in attendance were distinctly and obviously upper crust. Doc dined on sinfully delicious "gumbo," so thick he could almost stand the spoon in it. He was served warm, freshly baked croissants and enjoyed a single Sazerac, which he found a slender trace too heavy on the bitters, but he hesitated to complain to the waiter. He finished with a café au lait.

Outside, he bought a *Times-Democrat*. There was little news of crime, which, in a city saturated with it, seemed incredible. Two items only could be classified. There was a brief follow-up story on the most recent killing. The police were investigating; progress was being made; an arrest was expected soon. Ho-hum. Also, as a direct result of the eleven-corpse spree, a

Citizens Anti-Crime Committee of Fifty was being formed, boasting some of the most respected men in New Orleans. They were to assist the authorities in gathering evidence against the Mafia. Hennessey needed them about as much as he needed a third thumb, thought Doc ruefully.

He disposed of the paper in a convenient trash barrel and paused to consider his next move. He needed time to think the thing through carefully. He would go back to the hotel, lock himself in, and go to work. He would be meeting Raider at the Gate of the Two Lions in Toulouse Street at ten that evening. Raider would not be coming back to the Hotel Gregg; their split-up had to be complete, even to hanging their hats in separate districts after work. He planned to bring his partner's saddlebags to the meeting.

He got back to the hotel shortly before two. He was on his way up the stairs when the clerk, who was busy tossing letters into room pigeonholes, paused and called up to him.

"Fellow up theah waitin' foh you."

Doc stiffened. "Who?"

"Says his name's Hastings."

"Thanks."

He continued on up. Which Mr. Hastings, he wondered, George or Joe?

George opened to his knock, handing him his room key as he did so. He appeared very worried, nervous, fidgety. He cast a quick look up and down the hall, and, seizing his arm, practically pulled him into the room bodily. Quickly, he shut and bolted the door.

"Well, well, well," began Doc expansively.

"Ssssh, keep it down. These walls are as thin as paper. Sit down."

"Thanks, I will," rejoined Doc, amused. "What is this—have you changed your mind?"

"Let's just say we ought to talk a little more. You and me, not Joe. He'd come after me with a ball bat if he knew I was here. And not Hennessey. We keep him out o' this, I mean it."

"You don't trust him?"

"Trust got nothing to do with it. He's a good man, I guess. Honest. The trouble is he can't back up his word."

"You blame him for what happened to your brother?"

"Wouldn't you?"

He was sweating, noted Doc. His stomach had to be grinding into little pieces. This was probably the toughest thing he'd ever had to do in his life. He pitied him. What a way to have to live. What a town to live in.

Doc got out a cheroot, running it under his nose perfunctorily and screwing it into the corner of his mouth. "I really don't know who to blame. How about Peter himself?"

George bristled, his eyebrows snapping together over his nose like two furry beetles clashing. His jaw tightened. He started up from his chair.

"Take it easy," said Doc, "I'm not downing him or accusing him. But think about it, George. You know what goes on in this town. There's no such thing as a secret, not from the mob. It's even worse down on the docks. It's possible somebody overheard Peter. Or maybe he told somebody outright, someone he thought he could trust."

"Only me and Joe."

"Maybe somebody overheard you talking about it. One word, George, even a vague hint that Peter might have been just thinking of cooperating. Maybe not even that much, just the sight of Hennessey in your backyard, could have sent somebody running to the Matrangas."

"Hennessey didn't come to the docks. He's smarter than that."

"All I'm saying is it's almost impossible to keep a secret." He lit up and puffed. "You realize, of course, your brother wasn't killed just because he met with Hennessey. At that point, that early, he probably didn't know himself whether he'd go through with it. He could easily have backed out of any arrangement. What could Hennessey have done? But, and follow me closely on this, *when the Matrangas found out, they didn't warn him, they didn't wait until two days before the trial, they killed him*. Why? As a warning to you two, to keep you in line. Fairly effective device, wouldn't you say?"

"You saying we're yellow?"

"Of course not. You're in a corner. I know what you're up against. But you just can't blame Hennessey out of hand. Peter's getting killed had to be the last thing he wanted."

"He didn't protect him like he promised. And what's the

government going to do? What's the big plan?"

Doc winced inwardly, as if invisible fingers had pinched his conscience. What government? The Pinkertons hadn't had anything to do with the government since the Civil War. If George even suspected that he was lying, leading him on, he'd kill him with his bare hands. But the die was cast. There could be no backtracking now.

"I already told you what we're going to do, clean up New Orleans. Toss a net over the Delta. Some of them'll be hanged, those that don't hang will be put away for life. The rest will be deported, sent back to Sicily."

George stared at him without comment, without a murmur. Doc drew on the Old Virginia, sending a gauzy blue ring ceilingward, affecting nonchalance as best he could, the pose of one as certain of his power and control as a king on his throne.

"Okay," said George wearily, the voice of capitulation. "I'll give you everything: names, dates, places, the works. All you'll need to get the bastards, the Matrangas, Esposito, every one." He tapped his temple. "It's all in here."

"And you'll testify before the grand jury?"

He hesitated. He was still in the grip of his fear, still sweating, but he nodded.

"Let me get a pad and pencil."

"No! Not here, for chrissakes. You crazy?" He cast about. "I was stupid even to come here. That clerk downstairs has probably skinned out, run straight to Tony and Charlie."

"He hasn't, George. If he recognized you, he wouldn't have hung around until I got back, would he? Okay, you pick the time and the place."

"You know the woods out on the River Road, out past the swamp?"

"I can find them."

"Come tonight, ten o'clock. I'll be waiting off the road in a buggy. You be smoking one of those things, so I can see the glow, okay? So I'll know it's you."

Doc thought a moment, letting his words sink in. Ten o'clock would mean he would miss his meeting with Raider at the Gate of the Two Lions in Toulouse Street. But that was all right. He could leave him a sealed note at the desk. He'd be sure to come back to the hotel when he got tired of waiting. He'd word the note cleverly, something like: The cats can wait; we'll see them tomorrow. He'd read between the lines.

But there was something else.

"What's the matter?" George asked.

"Not a thing. Ten o'clock's fine. Only..." He paused, mentally bracing himself. "I'd like to bring Hennessey with me." George started to protest, shaking his huge head vigorously. Doc hurried his words, stopping him before he could start. "You've got to understand, we can't operate independently. The U.S. government always works with local law enforcement. Always. It's the best way, the only way."

George thought this over. "Okay, I guess. Only just Hennessey, not half the goddamn force."

"The River Road woods at ten o'clock sharp."

George eyed him appraisingly. "How much do you know about this mess?"

"Very little at this point, only what Hennessey and Sergeant Montaigne have told me."

He scoffed, dismissing this with a wave. "They don't know beans."

"Let me tell you something, George, before we go any further. David Hennessey is a dedicated man. He's been collecting evidence left and right. They've tried to kill him seven times, but that hasn't stopped him. Hasn't even slowed him down. He's got courage, he's smart, he works like a dog. All he needs is George Provenzano and he can nail the lid down on this thing. And you and your brother's troubles, and everybody else's, will be over."

Geroge grunted. "I'll believe it when I see it." He studied Doc. "You know any Italian?"

"No."

"Then you don't know what *pizzu* means. It means the beak of a little bird, like a canary, *capish?* When the mob squeezes money out of honest businessmen, out of madams and whores, anybody, they call it *fari vagnari a pizzu,* "wetting the beak," *capish?*" The bastards wet their beaks in everything, not just bananas and crotches. Anything that makes money they want a piece of. You pay every month on the first day." He rubbed his fingers together. "You know how they started with us?" He caught himself and looked from one wall to the other. "Never mind. It'll wait till tonight, right?"

He got up, stretching. "I got to get back. Joe'll be wondering what I'm up to. Christ, if he ever suspected, he'd kill me!"

He's going to have to know sooner or later, reflected Doc. "Is there a back way out downstairs?"

"I don't know."

"There must be. I'll find it."

He offered his hand. Doc shook it warmly. "You're doing the right thing, George. You're being smart."

"Smart, yeah, or..." He slit his throat with his finger, grinning weakly. "See you tonight."

Doc closed the door after him. He would have to go see Hennessy; they had to talk. Maybe this was the big break they were all hoping for. Ten o'clock would tell. Still, it looked much too easy a solution to such a complicated mess. Peter Provenzano had died. Would George follow him to the grave? Would he even make it to the River Road woods that night?

Why was he doing this? He had hesitated to ask him, to get into that aspect of the thing for fear that getting him thinking about it might change his mind.

Was it that he just wanted to get even for Peter? Or was it that he was sick and tired of the whole filthy business, of being slowly strangled by the Matrangas.

He stumped out his cheroot. Whatever his reasons...

"He's not going to die like his brother, damn it. We can't let that happen!"

CHAPTER FOUR

Raider wasn't overly fond of buying booze for strange floozies, despite the blossoming of his almost instantaneous fondness for Billy Cobb. At that, he thought, he could charge it to expenses, and honestly. It was legitimate, though he'd no doubt have to argue the old man and Bill Wagner out of reimbursement. Screw it.

He sat at a table, sipping bourbon, adding additional warmth to his stomach, which was already warmed by his meeting with Esposito. Opposite sat Mr. Hair's lady friend. Unbelievable, thought Raider, she was young enough to be the bastard's granddaughter, sweet as honey, beautiful, but something less than brilliant. In fact, if anything remotely resembling a brain rested between her pretty pink ears, nothing she had said so far was proof this was so.

He did not bring up Esposito. Why press his luck? Make friends, get into Dulcie Mae's confidence, if possible, then let the pearls fall or extract them, whichever. Billy was doing the talking, prattling on about a new pair of shoes she'd just bought.

The Bird Cage was loud and pretentious, little more than a garishly painted and gussied-up hole in the wall, he determined upon entering with his two new friends, spying and seizing a corner table. A Negro in a derby and peppermint-striped shirt sat at the piano in the opposite corner, flailing away. At the end of the piano was a dance floor, approximately the size of a manhole cover, but none of the patrons appeared interested in dancing. Looking around, as he took his seat, his back to the corner, he decided that most of those present were either drunk or on their way to it.

The ceiling was festooned with wax fruit, a bunch of grapes the size of a basketball hanging directly over his head. If they ever fell, they'd brain him, he thought. The walls were amateurishly painted with murals depicting horny-looking men with horns and goat bodies chasing lightly clad maidens. It had to be some kind of dance, he decided. One of the goat-men sat on a rock toodling his pipes. A large stain, where somebody had tossed a bottle, veiled the musician's face. The stink of disinfectant vied with Billy's lilac perfume.

"What's your line o' work, John?"

"I sell western gear—hats, boots, guns . . ."

"That why you're all dudded out like a cowhand?"

"That's it."

"How y'all 'spect to sell western duds in New Ohleans?"

"Oh man, I'm planning to open up a whole new market down here. Year from today you won't see a derby or fedora in town. I'll have ten-gallon hats on every head, right down to the tads."

"You're fulla shit. You're funny, though." Billy paused, angling her head, staring at him, winking, grinning. "I'n he cute, Dulcie? Cute as a brass button. How'd y'all like to go to bed free, John O'Toole? How'd y'all?"

"You don't beat round the bush, do you?" he said, feeling his cheeks color.

"The hell ah don't!" She burst out laughing. "I'll beat you to death, y'all see iffn' ah don't." Again she laughed, and sobered. "What'd y'all want to know 'bout Mr. E.?"

Raider cleared his throat. What the hell, he thought. Damn tooth had to be pulled; might as well jerk it out.

"He's the big money man in town, isn't he? Got his finger in lotsa pies."

"Ah'll tell the world. Y'all wanta meet him? Dulcie Mae'll introuduce y'all, won't you, honey?"

"Later, thanks. First I'd like to know 'bout him. Is it true if you want to do business in New Orleans you got to do business with him?"

"True as preachin'. Tell him, honey."

"What's to tell?"

Raider sighed inside. The look on her face gave her away. Mere mention of Esposito and she tightened up. She was obviously afraid of him. Afraid, hell! More like terrified. He probably beat her up daily, just to work up an appetite for breakfast. Son of a bitch! She *was* beautiful, friggin' ravishing. And so young. Little more than a child. In an instant his blood was boiling. What in red hell was a piece of dirt like Esposito doing coming within a city block of her, let alone pawing and fucking and abusing her?

"What the hell you want with an old man like that?" he burst out. "A damn criminal!"

Damn it! What the hell did he do that for? Stupid idiot! He expected her to snap back at him, but she didn't. She stared, her lovely eyes widening, her upper lip sneaking behind her lower, an abashed expression coming over her face.

"He's good to me. He gives me money. He buys me nice things."

Oldest story in the book, he thought. How in hell do you fight it? The door was open, the horse was out. He might just as well follow through.

"Dulcie Mae, let me say something." He lowered his voice and his head, bringing both their heads down into intimacy. "Your friend Giuseppe is a bad man, real bad. They don't come any worse. No, no, I know he's good to you, buys you things and suchlike, but he hurts people. Lots o' people. Tortures 'em, murders 'em. He's the Mafia, you know that. There's lots you know. He's *it* in this town, all wrapped up in one little buncha hate covered with hair. He's illegal, Dulcie, and because he is, the law's going to get him. They got to stop the blood, the killing. Got to rescue the city from the bastard. Ship him back to Sicily, him and his pals. All Chief Hennessey needs is evidence. You can help, little lady, mightily."

"Not me." Her hand went to her chest fearfully, and she shrank back in horror. "I couldn't. He'd . . . I couldn't do that."

"Somebody's got to, you know that."

"Somebody has, honey," said Billy, sipping and setting her glass down. And suddenly looking as serious as a nun, thought Raider admiringly. How nice it was having somebody new in his corner.

"I couldn't. I dasn't. 'Sides, I don't know nothin' 'bout his business."

Raider's expression was as threatening as he could make it. "You hear things. You see 'em. You see people. You're round when there's meetings."

"Sometimes." She caught herself, as if abruptly conscious that she was talking too much. She glanced furtively about the room. "I can't say nothin'. Please don't make me."

"Nobody's going to 'make' you," he said. "I'm just asking. In the name o' common decency. You know right from wrong. I'm asking on account it's right. In your heart you know it is. If I was your pappy or your maw sitting here saying so you'd be nodding your head. You know you would. You want to talk, you're purely bursting to, but you're 'fraid, isn't that so?"

She nodded.

"Then I'll tell you what. The police, Chief Hennessey, he'll take you under his wing, protect you. Fix it so nobody you don't want to can come within ten blocks o' you. Not Esposito, nobody. From now on. Better yet, he could fix it so you can leave town, go anyplace you please. You'll get money, all you'll need. All I'm asking is just think 'bout it. That can't hurt, can it? Think 'bout what you know, what Chief Hennessey needs to know. Think 'bout what you'd do if you were back home in Fulton County and I was your paw talking to you. If you were back there and he asked, you'd tell him, wouldn't you now. You'd spill every blessed bean."

He leaned forward as far as he could, tapping each single word out on the table. "On account it'd be right to do, proper, decent. Your conscience'd want you to. There wouldn't be any power on earth could keep you from talking. None." He straightened. "Think 'bout it, Dulcie, that's all I'm asking. Now relax, we'll say no more 'bout it. We'll just drink up, order 'nother round and enjoy ourselves. What do you two say I go over to that piano player, give him a shiny dime, and ask him to play 'The Jaybird and the Honeybee'? How 'bout it?"

The piano player professed not to know "The Jaybird and

the Honeybee." Not for a shiny dime. Billy's smudged quarter sparked his memory. She begged Raider to stay for another song and another after that. Dulcie Mae left. He was reluctant to stay, but not overly so; so long as she was spending her quarters. And he liked her company. He loved staring at her tits out of the corner of his eye. They set his mouth to watering and kept it moist. His admiration was not lost on her. If, he reasoned, a man's stare had any effect on a woman's tits, he thought, she and every other deliciously endowed female on earth would be flatter than the lid on a cigar box.

She got them to a room upstairs, pushing him protestingly inside.

"I got work to do, Billy. I got no time for playing tumble. Got no energy."

"Y'all won't need none."

She sat him down on the rickety iron bed, setting it squeaking painfully. She began to undress, doffing one piece of clothing after another as lightly, easily, and effortlessly as if she were pulling petals from a flower. The roseate glow of the night-table lamp gave her flawless skin a pinkish hue. He swallowed hard, unable to wrench his eyes from the awesome and absorbing display. Within seconds, she was standing naked as an egg before him. She moved close. She lifted his hand, laving his outstretched fingers with her warm, moist tongue and sliding them down onto her breast. She pushed her breast into his mouth. He thrashed it softly and sucked and she pushed and pushed, forcing as much as she could into his mouth. She accorded the other breast the same brief pleasure, then set about readying him for what was to come.

Within moments, without words, without lengthy preliminaries, without anything except the necessary preparations, she was down on the bed and he was on top. She was right, he thought fleetingly, about his not having to expend any appreciable degree of energy. He held fast and she did the fucking, the bucking, pushing, grinding. Engorging his throbbing manhood, vising it at the root, all but ripping it off. She fucked like a queen mink in scalding heat. He could only groan and suffer and enjoy, feeling his balls load to the hardness of ball-peen hammer heads and explode. Fear hurtled through his mind: His cock had split eye to base, like a banana neatly halved to receive the ice cream, the cream, and the nuts and cherries . . .

When it was over, when the jouncing had stopped and she rested panting, catching her breath, sweat beading her upper lip, cheeks, and forehead, he withdrew. It was with cautious restraint. He dreaded the sight of his cock, certain that if not split, at the very least it would come out battered beyond recognition, black and blue and bloody. It did not.

Raider's antagonist, the waitress-whore, had no name, none she cared to volunteer for Doc's edification. Thirty seconds after George Provenzano left the room, a knock sounded and Doc opened the door to her grinning presence.

"'Lo."

"Hello," he said, gulping, striving unsuccessfully to keep his eyes from rounding in admiration and his Adam's apple from jumping out of his throat. She was a big one, in every respect, at every corner and contour.

"Can I come in?"

He nodded, suppressing a second gulp. In she sailed, skirts swishing, pushing the delicate fragrance of heather, he guessed it to be, before her, divesting herself daintily of her gloves and her feather-infested hat, which was outrageously large and sprawling—nearly as huge if not as heavy as a washbasket riding a laundress's head.

"I want to fuck you," she said sweetly.

"Well, I . . ."

"I know, this is so sudden. That's the way it goes sometimes, right? I like you. Did from the first I laid eyes on you. Don't like your friend. He's a shit-kicking goat, but you're a gentleman. I can see that. Look good, nice smile, smell good. Just relax." She sat him on the end of the bed and began unbuttoning his fly.

"Wait a minute . . ."

"Can't. Time's wasting. Got a big night ahead of me. But pleasure before business." She laughed lightly.

She got his cock out and began working it hard, stiff as a rail spike, purpling, throbbing, all within not more than fifteen seconds. Down on her knees she went, flaying it with her tongue, running the tip of it down the under, tender side, pulling down his trousers, getting at his balls, nipping them, biting lightly, swabbing them with her tongue.

"Oh, my Lord," he murmured. "Welcome to New Orleans."

Slurp. "Welcome..." Slurp. "New Orleans..."

She did not disrobe. Did not bother. Instead, pulling up her skirts, she revealed her coal-black quim, pulling the pink lips apart, baring it wet and steaming, ready for cock, hungry for it, craving.

"Oh, my Lord..."

Submissively, like a sheep going to the slaughter, he mounted her, spread her legs and pushed home. To his chagrin, he mentally, bodily followed his cock into the pink, wet vastness of her quim. The lips closed behind him.

* * *

Billy ate him with such abandon, such incredible enthusiasm and energy, he was amazed that she did not swallow him whole. It was, as she put it, "Mommy's way of making him well," reducing the pain of their fuck, restoring something like normalcy to his battered pride. Ringing his cock, she swung lightly up and down it, her lips barely touching, the lubrication of her saliva combined with the drippings of his previous come rendering the action supremely comfortable, the effect immensely enjoyable. Down and up, down and up, her relentless tongue swirling and swabbing, gently abusing, filling his balls, setting them silently rumbling.

He came, groaning, lighting her face with a broad, bright smile of satisfaction. She took the last errant drop into her mouth with the tip of her tongue, rolling the swallow from cheek to cheek, tilting her head back, her swollen tongue emerging, the come slithering down her throat.

"Deeeeeee...licious."

Again he groaned.

"That was fun; now let's get into some serious fucking!"

"For chrissakes no! No, no, no!"

Alas, the lady would not take no for an answer.

* * *

"That'll be ten dollars," said the waitress-whore.

"Ten? Are you serious?"

"I gave you the ten-dollar special. You look in the mirror at your face and tell me it wasn't worth it. Go ahead, look."

"I haven't got ten dollars," he lied.

"How much you got?"

"Three. Why don't I give you an I.O.U. for the balance? It's good as gold, my I.O.U. I get paid the end of the month."

She considered this, her dull eyes fastened on the wall. She nodded. The deal was completed. She left. He lay back on the bed, smiling through his heartfelt sigh.

"Shame on you, Weatherbee. Shame, shame!" He winced in pain, sucking in his breath sharply. On second thought, who was taking advantage of whom?

CHAPTER FIVE

Church bells pealed solemnly, sounding the quarter hour. Raider continued pacing back and forth in front of the Gate of the Two Lions in Toulouse Street. The fronds of an overhanging banana tree rustled just above his head as the soft, warm breeze invaded them, bringing with it the fragrance of oleander. A young couple was sitting on the balcony above the door beyond where he paced. Above the Gate of the Two Lions the two stone beasts rested, facing one another, holding down the wall pillars, holding up the gates. Raider could make out their dim outlines against the star-strewn darkness.

Back and forth he paced, his patience deserting him. He swore softly to himself, then began talking, then arguing, trotting out a dozen different reasons for the delay in Doc's arrival.

"Son of a bitch is dead. For sure. Throat slit and lying in some goddamn alley. Goddamn town! I purely hate this place. Everybody on the take, everybody on the make. Goddamn sinkhole!"

44

The bells announced half past ten. Off he marched, mumbling irritably, hands jammed in his pockets, head down, crossing Orleans Alley and turning left at Chartres in the direction of Jackson Square. He needed a drink. Not damn bourbon; Scotch, something with taste to it. One, maybe three, then back to the Hotel Gregg. Doc'd be there. If he wasn't he'd leave word with the clerk. He wouldn't do this, just up and not show up . . .

Not unless he was lying in some goddamn alley with his throat painting his vest red. General Jackson, still bronze, still astride his bronze horse, still charged untiringly, observed and attended by few passersby and a host of pigeons, eyed him blindly as he passed. He came within sight of the Bird Cage. It was lit with Japanese lanterns and crammed with patrons. He was within ten steps of the place when a familiar voice called to him.

"John!"

Not called so much as barked. Billy came running, her skirts swishing, beads jangling, fire in her eyes.

"Where in hell y'all been? I been lookin' all ovah! I figured y'all'd come back."

"Hold it, hold it, simmer down, for chrissakes. What you got, a hornet up your—"

"John, Dulcie's been killed! Murdered!"

"WHAT!"

"Just 'bout."

"She's alive?"

"But beat up so her face looks like a half watahmelon dropped on a rock. Every bone in her body busted, just 'bout."

"Where is she?"

"I got a couple friends to take her to St. Joseph's. That's closest to where it happened."

"Who did it? As if I had to ask."

"You, you son of a bitch. You talking to her, being seen with her. It was all he needed. Somebody saw and told him." She paused, glaring. "You're some kinda law, ain't you? You are, y'all got to be!"

"That's bullshit. I told you what I do."

"You fibbing me? If you are, I swear I'll cut your balls off. I will! I love that little girl. She's my baby sister. I talked and talked to her 'bout busting up with him, practically pleaded on bended knee. She wouldn't listen. Oh, she'd listen, even nod her head yes, but she was 'fraid to, scared shiverin'."

"Never mind. Let's get over there."

St. Joseph's Hospital was an eerie, cavernous tomb by night, its too few lamps glowing feebly, barely able to dispel the pitch blackness creeping in through the high, shadeless windows, its ceilings lofty and vaulted, painted a funereal gray, cracked and peeling. Footsteps clicked and echoed on the stone floor, and whispers resembled muffled shouting, carrying upward and reverberating from the ceiling. A nun, sitting at the reception desk, her cowled head bent over a chart, her slender, waxen finger tracing line after line, looked up and smiled a greeting as Raider and Billy approached. Raider circled his hat brim self-consciously, feeling for all the world as if he were about to enter the catacombs in quest of the bones of his ancestors, and that this frail, pleasant, wimpled little woman was to be his guide down long, dank, and drafty tunnels to burial vaults sequestered and unseen for centuries.

He shivered slightly and licked his lips. Bill spoke briefly to the sister. She was given a card. They ascended to the second floor, passing a niche occupied by the Holy Mother holding the Christ child. On the wall ahead of them where the stairway turned, hung a large crucifix, the light from a lamp above it descending to illuminate Christ's crown of thorns and his forehead, face, and shoulders. Raider noticed and looked away, swinging to his right, following Billy up to the second floor.

They passed partially opened doors, patients lying in silence, an old woman with her head and face heavily bandaged, saying her rosary, a man in traction, four patients sharing a room, dutifully ignoring one another, passing their times of pain in the privacy of their thoughts. The abject dismalness of the place, the unrelenting dreariness struck him as the strongest possible barrier to recovery, a device to delay, to forestall restoration of the body by effectively depressing the mind and heart.

A nun sat in the corridor reading a small black book. She looked up as they approached, smiling, holding out her hand for the card the receptionist had given Billy. She nodded toward a door on the left at the end. She was attractive, thought Raider, just about Billy's age, fresh, scrubbed, and shiny-looking, gleaming forehead and cheeks with natural roses. But her lips were as pale as death.

Two women, he thought, the same age, same degree of beauty, same warmth and goodness of heart from two different worlds, worlds as separate and distinct one from the other as the sun and moon. Two different paths taken early and followed to two different endings—one sinful, one holy, a life freely given to God, dedicated in unswerving allegiance to Him.

He wondered what was going on in Billy's mind as the nun directed them. Was she comparing herself to her? Was she self-conscious in her presence? Did she feel shame, guilt? She, Billy, looked intensely serious, an expression he had never seen on her face before, a solemnness he would never have imagined her capable of. Did the nun realize what she was? Did *she* compare them? Was she judging Billy? Did she pity her?

They moved on. The nun closed her book, got up, and followed them. She went ahead and opened the door. Dulcie Mae lay with her eyes closed. For a split second Raider thought that there was only her head, set deep in the pillow, that she had no body, so nearly flat were the covers. Both eyes were black and blue, one cheek hugely swollen, puffed up like the belly of a bird, he thought pityingly. Her face was covered with lacerations and her head was bandaged, a strip of gauze framing her battered face and supporting her chin.

The nun preceded them into the room, standing aside.

"Dr. Gireaux has given her morphine for the pain. She is not fully awake. That is, she is hazy. It is difficult for her to speak, you understand. No more than a few minutes, please. And do not say anything to upset her, that might make her move involuntarily. I will come back."

"She gonna make it okay?" Raider asked.

The nun nodded. "Most of her wounds are superficial. But painful. Two ribs were broken and her shoulder dislocated, but it has been set."

"Will her face..." began Billy.

"There will be a scar on her chin and her mouth." She

indicated the corners of her own. "They will fade in time. She is lucky."

Billy gaped. "Lucky?"

"She was brutally beaten. She could easily have died."

"How long she gonna have to be here?" asked Raider.

"Ten days, perhaps two weeks. You'll have to ask the doctor."

"Is he around?"

"I think he is downstairs in the isolation ward. Ask Sister Theresa at the desk when you leave."

"Thank you, Sister," said Billy.

The nun stood with her hand on the doorknob. "No more than a few minutes. She is very tired, very uncomfortable."

She closed the door. Billy leaned over one side, Raider the other.

"Honey, it's me."

Dulcie Mae tried to smile, wincing with the effort. "Billy . . ."

"He did this, right?" murmured Raider.

Dulcie Mae turned her head slightly, her eyes reacting, discovering his presence.

"Mmm."

"What for?"

"For being seen with y'all," snapped Billy testily.

"That's all, that's it, just us being seen together. You didn't tell me a blessed thing, nothing. But he doesn't care 'bout that. Somebody sees us, goes running to him, you go back to him loyal as can be, not a word to me, and this is what he gives you. He coulda killed you."

"John, shut up!" rasped Billy. "Stop pickin' on her."

"I'm not, goddamn it. I'm making a goddamn point!"

"Hush up that cussin'!"

"Shut up, Billy. We got no time for nonsense. We got to talk. Don't interrupt. Dulcie, I meant what I said to you this afternoon. Every word gospel. I can get you protection. The son of a bitch'll never get close to you again. Just say the word. Just nod. Chief Hennessey'll put two o' the biggest, toughest cops on the force outside your door, and the only body'll get in here'll be your doctor and the sisters. That son of a bitch Esposito so much as shows his hairy face at the front door, they'll bust him in half. I give you my solemn word on it."

"Listen to him, honey, he's making' good sense. He's done this to y'all afore, but this is the worst eveh, ain't that so? Next time'll be the last, next time..."

Dulcie Mae's eyes were flooding with fear. "Want to get 'way. 'Fraid..."

"Course you are," said Raider. "Who wouldn't be? But we can fix things so you'll never have to be afraid again, ever. Not as long as you live. I swear to God Almighty. I can have two policemen up here in fifteen minutes. Just say the word."

There was a long, weighty silence. Raider could hear his heartbeat increasing its pace as his expectations rose. The breeze rattled the window, and Dulcie Mae shifted her weight slightly under the covers. She wet her lips. A deep, livid cut started from the center of her lower lip, crossing it at an angle, continuing down to the side of her chin, vanishing under the bandage supporting her chin. Stitching showed like tiny tracks on either side of it.

"Say yes, honey," said Billy, her tone appealing, pleading. "Please, Dulcie."

Dulcie Mae tried to nod. "Yes," she whispered. "I'll do what you want."

Billy grinned. "That's mah girl."

Raider straightened. "Stay here, Billy."

"Ah can't. Y'all heard the sister."

"Not in the room, outside the door. I'm going to the station. I'll get Hennessey to detail a couple o' men. You plant yourself outside that door."

It opened. The nun stuck her head in.

"Okay, okay," said Raider. "We're leaving. Only, the lady here is gonna stay outside, okay?"

"I don't understand..."

He explained. The nun nodded slowly. "I will see that two chairs are brought up for them."

"They'll be here afore you know it."

He left, walking as fast as he could down the hall, running down the stairs and out into the night.

"Donahue and Forzaglia are two good, reliable boys," said Frank Montaigne, finishing pouring coffee, proffering the tin cup to Raider. "They'll take good care of her. She's being smart. Her worries are oveh, and the mob's are just beginning. You've corraled us an ace, Raidah."

"I should be getting back."

"Stick around a few minutes. They know the way. Relax. Nobody'll get neah her with those two on the doah."

"Where's Hennessey?"

"Gone to meet your partner."

They were sitting in the chief's office. The sergeant reassumed his chair and repositioned his feet on the desk, the snaps of his suspenders catching the light of the radiant wall lamp, momentarily dazzling Raider.

"So that's why Doc never showed up," he said.

He sipped. Montaigne could make interesting conversation, he thought, but not coffee. It tasted like mud, and so strong it set his teeth on edge. He set the cup down.

"What's going on with those two?"

"Dave didn't say, only that he was heading out River Road to make a meet, and that Weathahbee'd be theah."

"Who else?"

Montaigne shrugged. He cocked his head. "What you got there?"

Raider pulled out Esposito's gun and handed it over. "Present for you. From the big Mafioso."

Montaigne's eyes widened. "This is Esposito's?"

"Was. I took it off him. Little boys shouldn't play with big guns."

The sergeant was examining it. "This is a damn cannon. Must weigh fouh pounds. Made in Belgium. Eleven-seventy-five millimeters. I've nevah seen anything like it."

"Damn forty-five cartridge'd rattle like a pea in a tin can in that barrel. I'm surprised the little bastard could lift it, let alone shoot the fucking thing."

Montaigne dropped it on the desk. "We'll stick it in ouh gun weapons museum up on the second floah. How the hell did you get it away from him?"

"Swapped him one o' my boots. How do you think? I got the drop on him. Got his pig sticker, too."

He produced Esposito's knife, tossing it clinking lightly on the desk. Then he changed his mind and retrieved it.

"I think I'll hang on to it. Souvenir."

Montaigne laughed. "Maybe you'll get a chance to cut his throat." He lowered his legs and drew his chair close. "How'd you find him? How'd you get the drop on him?"

Raider got to his feet, putting his hat back on. "I'll tell you the whole story, only not now. I really got to get back to the hospital."

"They don't need you. Come on, Raidah, tell me what happened."

"Another time, Frank. Look, if Weatherbee should come back with Hennessey, tell him I was by, and I'll be back, okay? We got to touch bases."

"I have no ideah when they'll be back."

"If. So long. Careful o' that fieldpiece. Don't go blowing your foot off."

"You'h something, you know that, Pink?"

"Course I know. Don't I keep telling myself?"

He ran all the way back to St. Joseph's, cursing himself for lingering at the station. Donahue and Forzaglia could be the best two cops in the world, it still didn't allay his concern. The damn town was as wide open as a burned barn.

"Every time you turn round, somebody else gets it. Bloodiest damn place I've ever seen."

He passed two old women walking a runty dog. All three stared at him, talking to himself. Billy spotted him from the hospital doorway. He ran up to her, panting. She was crying into a sodden ball of hanky.

"What's the matter?"

"She's dead, that's what's the matter! Son of a bitch, damn!"

He stared aghast. "You're kidding!"

"Yeah, I'm kidding, you horse's ass!"

"How? She . . ."

"Murdered, how do y'all think? He sneaked in and cut her throat, poor sweet, innocent kid. Nevah harmed a soul, never. It was horrible!"

"Who, for chrissakes!"

He had her by the upper arms and was shaking her.

"The doctor . . ."

"Gireaux?"

"Some intern, think it was. Ah don't know. Ah was standing

outside like y'all said. Sister Elizabeth was down the hall in her chair reading, and this fellow come up. He looked like a doctor, dressed like one, y'all know. He had one o' them things you stick in your ears to listen to somebody's heart."

"Did he say anything?"

"Said 'lo. He was good-lookin', blond, blue eyes. Ah said hello back. He just went inside, closed the door, and come out a few seconds aftah. He said she's gonna be fine, temperature's down. Oh, dear, sweet God in heaven, John, why did he kill her? Why? She nevah harmed a livin' soul."

"To shut her up," muttered Raider morosely. "Why do you think?"

"She nevah said nothin'."

"Esposito doesn't know that. He had to be sure. When did the cops get here? Too late, I know, but when exactly?"

"What cops?"

"Oh, for chrissakes, don't tell me."

He heard laughter. He turned. Donahue and Forzaglia were coming up the street, one laughing, pushing the other playfully in the shoulder. They recognized Raider, both sobering at the sight of him.

"Hi-yah, bucko," said Donahue. He was beefy, broad-shoul-dered, well and artistically scarred, with a voice that sounded like it was rising from the bottom of a well.

"You're too late. Somebody got to her. She's dead," said Raider flatly.

Billy pushed him, so hard she all but toppled him where he stood. "It's your fault, you bastard, you stinkin' son of a bitch! If y'all hadn't a gone an' pushed yourself into her life this wouldn'ta happened. Y'all cut her throat!" She whirled on the two officers. "He did, just as much as if he held the knife hisself. Bastard! Son of a bitch!"

"Here, here, little miss, calm down," said Forzaglia.

"Y'all go to hell, cop. Let go o' me."

Wrenching free of his hold, she ran off, sobbing loudly, uncontrollably. Forzaglia started after her. Raider stayed him.

"Let her go. Where you two been, anyways?"

They exchanged glances.

"We stopped off at Shaugnessey's Ale House," said Donahue. "We hadn't eaten."

"Montaigne told you to get over here fast, didn't he?"

"We only stopped a couple minutes," said Forzaglia sheepishly.

"That's all it took, goddamn it! Jesus Christ, if you two are the best on the force, I'd hate like hell to see the worst."

"You want we should go up and check things out?" asked Forzaglia. He got his pad and pencil out of his pocket.

"Check it out," said Raider wearily. "I'm going back to the station."

CHAPTER SIX

The peepers, tree frogs, and other night creatures were hard at it, the din swelling and ebbing through the thick stands of oak encircled by curly pine. It was as black as the inside of his derby, mused Doc, sitting on a stump, extinguishing his cheroot between his knees. The foliage overhead blotted out the moon and stars completely.

Hennessey and George Provenzano towered over him. The banana importer was even more nervous than he'd been in the hotel room, observed Doc. He was pacing back and forth, pounding his massive fist into his palm, starting at every strange sound, and barking his answers to Hennessey's questions.

The chief was maintaining an enviable calm, reflected Doc, listening to the two of them. They had arrived just before ten, and George had shown up a few minutes after, driving his buggy off the road as far into the woods as he could. Hennessey paused in his questioning.

"George, take it easy, you're getting all worked up."

"Damned right I am. Wouldn't you be? I musta been nuts

to come out here. I'm as good as dead, you know that? You two got any idea what it feels like?"

"Listen to me. Nobody's coming after you, nobody's going to know where to find you. I've got it all figured out."

"Wonderful."

"I'm serious. I've got a summer place near Mandeville on Lake Pontchartrain. Beautiful spot. You'll be as safe there as if you were in your mother's arms. I'll give you two good men for bodyguards, the best men on the force, Joe Forzaglia and Dennis Donahue. They can lick their weight in wildcats. They're straight as a die."

"Forzaglia?"

"Italian. I know, I know. I've got dozens of Italian policemen. In this war they make the best troops. They hate the Mafia. Listen to me, the three of you can catch the midnight train. You'll have to change at Slidell. It's about twenty miles northwest of Slidell. You get off at Mandeville and walk back about half a mile. Dennis knows where it is." He held up a key. "There's fishing gear, a rowboat, a canoe. It's stocked with food, all the comforts." He pressed the key into George's hand.

"I don't know, Chief."

"We'll head back to town after we're done here. I'll introduce you to the boys, you head over to the railroad station, and off you go."

"I guess . . ." George grinned.

"Did I say something funny?" Hennessey asked.

"I was just thinking o' Joe. He's gonna think I disappeared off the face o' the earth. You got another man you can really trust, you send him over to our place and tell him, okay?"

"I don't think that's a good idea," said Doc.

"I don't either," said Hennessey.

"Come on, you're talking about my brother. I mean Joe . . ."

Hennessey laid a hand on his shoulder, stopping his pacing. "We're not pointing the finger at Joe."

"You goddamn better not!"

"Take it easy."

"You take it easy! I don't like that kinda talk."

Doc stood up. "What the chief's trying to say is this game is for keeps. The whole idea is to protect you. It's in our best interests to. You're our sleeve ace. What you've got to understand is that the chief knows what he's doing. You do as we suggest and you'll come out just fine. But if you tell Joe you're leaving and where you're going, who knows what'll happen? Oh, he's not going to blab it. But who knows, he could talk in his sleep. He might, God forbid, get kidnapped; get worked over..."

"They'd squeeze him till he popped," said Hennessey evenly. "Bleed it out of him."

George grunted. "What about my wife and kids?"

"Your family will be told you've gone into hiding for your protection," said Hennessey. "We can tell your brother that much, if you insist."

"I insist."

"I'll tell him. I'll tell your wife. Trust me, George, you've got to trust me. My word of honor. I'll do what's right." He paused and eyed him. "Let's go back to work. You were talking about the Matrangas muscling in."

"They first come around a couple years ago, the two o' them. They told us straight out, get off the docks. How do you like that for gall, eh? Pack up and get the hell outta here. Only Radzo stuck in his two cents."

"Radzo?" asked Doc.

"Esposito. That's a name he used to use when he first got here," explained Hennessey.

George went on. "He rented a house on Chartres Street, the big brick one with the ivy around the front door. He bought a lugger and got into the oyster trade between New Orleans and the lower coast. For a cover, you know? Meanwhile, he knocks off Tony Labruzzo, lines up all the small fry, and practically overnight he's in control o' the whole town. Anyway, when the Matrangas try to boot us off the docks, Esposito puts the thumb on it, stops 'em cold."

"Good man," said Doc kiddingly.

George glared and spit. "Not good, just not *stupido*. He figures we're successful because we know what we're doing, *capish*? Why ring in a buncha monkeys to run a business that's already running good? What you do is tie strings around the guys in charge so when you jerk the strings they jump. So the Matrangas don't push us out and move in, they just take over, if you understand the difference. Back then we had about seven hundred guys unloading for us, mostly blacks and *paisans*. They made us fire our guys and hire theirs. Pretty soon it was half theirs, half ours. Then they cut the wages from forty cents to a dime. The guys squawk like hell, so they up it a nickel. Fifteen cents an hour, when before they were making forty an hour days, sixty nights. And from me, Joe, and Peter the Matrangas collect the first of every month: a quarter o' the profits, then a third, now it's almost half. They're *stupido*, they're squeezing the cow to death, you follow me?"

"Doesn't Esposito know what's going on?" Doc asked.

"He doesn't care, not anymore. He's too busy with other things. He's into so much now, making so much money with the women, extortion, robbery, he couldn't care less about bananas. Tony and Charlie pay him his cut and tell him nothing, and he doesn't ask."

He fixed Hennessey with sober, beseeching eyes. "But if you can nail Espo to the cross, the whole operation'll collapse. Without him, the Mafia in New Orleans'd be like a snake without a head. Everybody'd start spilling their guts to protect themselves. The Matrangas, Manny Politz, Pietro Monasterio, Bastion Incardona, Tony Bagnetto—everybody'd go down the hole."

"That's precisely what we want to do, George, nail Esposito with enough to finish him off. And with your help, we can do it." Hennessey clapped him on the shoulder, a gesture of re-assurance. But the look on George's face told Doc that he didn't appreciate it, even though he didn't pull free.

How could he divest himself of guilt, of self-consciousness; how could he generate any enthusiasm for this, he thought? He was squealing like a common stool pigeon, a nickel-and-dime grifter, talking himself blue in the face for three dollars and a railroad ticket out of town. "Disgoosting necessoties," was what Allan Pinkerton called informers, and George Provenzano's personal opinion of such types probably wasn't even that high.

Still, in spite of how he must feel, in spite of his fears for his life, his brother, his family, his future, everything he had worked for and wanted hanging in the balance, he *was* talking, pouring out pertinent specifics in quantity, along with bitter recollections and juicy gossip. Would he continue to talk? Would he ultimately testify under oath before a grand jury?

Would he stand up before his friends and enemies and drive the nails into Esposito's palms and insteps? Or would he change his mind, back out, and leave them with an empty sack, forced to start all over again from scratch?

Doc searched George's eyes. There was no clue. How he privately felt about what he was doing, the depth of his commitment, his sincerity—they were his secret, securely locked in his heart.

CHAPTER SEVEN

Raider was waiting for them in Hennessey's office when the three returned from their get-together in the River Road woods. Donahue and Forzaglia had taken a statement from Sister Elizabeth and had turned in their report on the murder. They had searched the hospital for the blond, blue-eyed doctor but failed to find him. They did find a pair of trousers, a shirt, and a stethoscope bundled into a wastebasket in the third-floor lavatory, suggesting that Dulcie Mae's killer had evidently left the premises by way of the roof.

"He was no doubt standing on the damn roof watching the four of us down on the sidewalk talking," said Raider, his tone tinged with irony.

While he had been explaining to Hennessey what had happened at St. Joseph's, the chief periodically eyed George Provenzano, who was sitting in a corner. Clearly, mused Doc, looking on, Hennessey was concerned over what effect news of the girl's brutal murder would have on his star witness. Doc was mildly surprised that the chief permitted Raider to continue

59

his explanation within range of George's hearing.

"Eleven, twelve," observed Hennessey laconically, when Raider was finished. "Murder by the dozen. Frank..."

"Yes, Dave?"

"Go find Donahue and Forzaglia. Tell them to wait by the front door. They're going to be catching the midnight train up to Slidell with Mr. Provenzano here. Shake it up. They've only got about twenty minutes."

Montaigne nodded and left.

Raider's face assumed an expression of amazement. He shot a quick glance at George in the corner and frowned quizzically at Hennessey.

"Are you kidding?"

"What's the matter?" asked the chief.

"You're gonna give this fella those two jackasses for bodyguards?"

"Rade..." began Doc.

"Who you calling jackasses, mister? Officers Donahue and Forzaglia are two of our finest uniforms. Top men."

"Oh for chrissakes..."

"Rade..."

Doc shot to his feet, grabbed Raider by the elbow, and shoved him out into the hallway, slamming the door behind them.

"What the hell you doing?" Raider snapped, freeing his elbow.

"Will you shut your big mouth? Provenzano's already so tightened up he's on the verge of bursting a blood vessel. He's not interested in your opinion of those two. Nobody is."

"You damn well should be! They screwed up for fair. They were in some damn whoop-up swilling booze when they shoulda been at the hospital. The two of 'em smelled like a busted whiskey barrel when they come up to Billy and me on the street. If they'da been there when they should'a been, the girl'd still be alive!"

"You don't know that."

Raider started to respond, and stopped. He didn't "know that," but the realization failed to stem his ire. All that mattered was that a human being, a child, had been needlessly, brutally murdered. Beaten up, then murdered. And *he*, not Donahue and Forzaglia, was at fault. If he'd stayed away from her, if

Billy Cobb had kept him away . . . No, he couldn't blame Billy, even though she blamed him. There was no sharing this responsibility; it was all his. Billy was right.

"Irish asshole's screwing this thing up for fair, sending his star witness into hiding with those two misfits!"

"Shut up, Rade, he can hear you."

"Who the hell cares?"

Frank Montaigne came out with George, walking him down the hallway toward the front doors. Hennessey drifted out, his eyes narrowing at Raider, his cheeks reddening slightly. Doc sighed softly.

"You've got a big mouth, mister," said the chief evenly.

"You go to hell, *mister!*"

"Rade . . ."

Hennessey waggled a big finger in Raider's face, scowling darkly as he did so. "You watch your mouth. I'm not interested in your opinions. I don't want to hear 'em. I don't have to defend my men against your bullshit."

"You may goddamn have to when they screw up with him like they did with that little girl."

"Rade, shut up," pleaded Doc.

Hands on hips, Hennessey closed to within an inch of Raider, glowering, his voice assuming a rusty edge. "Listen to your partner, Mr. Shitkicker, he's giving you sound advice."

"Who you calling shitkicker, you mick son of a bitch!"

Before Doc could intervene, Raider shoved Hennessey. Hard. The chief's eyes widened and hardened, glowing fiercely. His rapidly reddening neck bulged, threatening to snap his collar button. His cheeks flushed. His lower lip quivered. Up came one meaty hand, flattening against Raider's face, pushing him back against the door. Raider countered, swinging wildly, his right glancing off the bigger man's shoulder with just enough force to start him spinning. Hennessey caught himself and came back with a hard left to the gut. Raider doubled over, whooshing loudly, cursing.

"Sucker-punching son of an Irish bitch!"

"Raider, for Christ's sakes!" exclaimed Doc.

They were suddenly toe to toe, cursing, belting away, bringing heads out of doorways. Frank Montaigne came running back. He wedged between Hennessey and Raider. Doc joined the effort.

But Raider was furious, and Hennessey even more so. And they were both much too powerful for the sergeant and Doc. Hennessey missed cleanly with a shot to Raider's head, his fist shattering the glass in the office door. He pulled back, bleeding, swearing vilely. About to counter with a left to the chest, following two successful smashes in the same general area, Raider froze, his attention seized by the sound of the glass. He gaped at the door. Hennessey came at him, slamming his bloodied fist against Raider's eye. Raider hit the wall behind him and slumped to his knees. Doc and the sergeant got between them. Montaigne turned, draping himself over his superior, pushing him away. Doc knelt beside Raider.

"You stupid idiot . . ."

"Shut your goddamn mouth. You got no business stickin' your nose in my business!"

"You're going to have yourself one beautiful shiner. Lovely." Raider ignored him. He was working his jaw, testing it gingerly with his bloodied fingertips. "Is it broken?"

"Feels like it is."

"GET HIM THE FUCK OUT OF HERE!" roared Hennessey, struggling to free himself of Montaigne's hold. "GET HIM OUT BEFORE I KILL THE SON OF A BITCH!"

Doc helped Raider to the front door, supporting him with one arm, opening the inner, then the outer door with the other. Raider sucked deep, drinking in the fresh air.

"Go back to the hotel," said Doc. "I'll be back in a little while. Don't worry, I'll work on him, smooth things over . . ."

"Screw him! You don't say a damn thing, not on my account. This is my squawk. It's none o' your goddamn business! He's screwing up, Doc—left, right, and through the middle. That's why he's so hair-triggered and short goddamned fused!"

"Rade, if you were Irish and somebody called you a son of an Irish bitch, you might not take it with a smile."

"So I mouthed off. So I was mad."

"Go back and wait for me."

"Screw you. I'm finished with this bullshit, I'm leaving town."

"Go ahead, sneak out when the going gets rough."

"You go to hell!"

"You can't leave till tomorrow, Rade, there're no more trains."

"I'll rent me a goddamn horse."

He pulled free, continuing to work his jaw tentatively. He investigated his eye and winced, hissing sharply, cursing under his breath.

And away he stalked.

"That is one beautiful one y'all got yourself there, friend," said the bartender through a sinister smile and rotten teeth. "What'll you have, bourbon or beefsteak?"

"All I want is information," said Raider grumpily. "Where's Billy Cobb?"

He glanced around the Bird Cage. It was past midnight and the late crowd was coming in. The piano player got up from his bench and was talking animatedly with a bosomy blonde, all sequins and feathers and ratty looking hair. The Japanese lanterns interspersed among the clusters of fruit, festooning the ceiling collectively, cast a feeble yellow glow down upon the faces and bald heads.

"Working, I guess," said the bartender.

"Where would that be?"

Again the sinister grin. The man licked his lips, wiped the bar, and pointed at it. Raider grunted and laid down a paper dollar.

"Emma Pickett's. Numbah twenty-five John Street. Between Gravier and Perdido. Think y'all can find it?"

Raider nodded, by now thoroughly disgusted with life, and even more so with the wiseacre behind the bar, who was at the moment appropriating his paper dollar. He folded it with exaggerated neatness and jammed it into his vest pocket.

"You a friend o' Billy's? I recollect seein' you in heah with her and Dulcie Mae."

"I'm her son," responded Raider dryly.

"Oh, funny man. Funny man with a funny hat. And funny eye. Ha, ha, ha . . ."

Raider bristled, leaned across the bar, grabbed a handful of shirt, and with his free hand deftly extracted his dollar from the offending one's pocket.

"Ha ha yourself, horseface."

"Leggo, I didn't mean nothing!"

Raider left, followed by all eyes. His own was beginning to close as the swelling increased. It took him better than half an hour to find 25 John Street. Admitted by a tuxedoed Negro servant, he waited in the spacious front room. He whistled softly, admiringly. Billy Cobb evidently worked fairly high up the ladder. The room was filled with mahogany and black walnut woodwork and furniture, oriental rugs, silver door-knobs, a carved marble fireplace, paintings, and statuary. No beaded curtains, no stinking cheap perfume. There was even a grand piano gracing one corner.

A barrel of a woman with a purple ostrich feather waving from her bright red hair and sufficient makeup plastered across her fat face to accommodate a circus clown came floating in.

"Good evening, good evening, good evening, Mr. . . ."

"Wilson."

"Mr. Wilson."

She cocked her head and eyed him appraisingly. The skin above and separating her massive breasts was red and stippled like a chicken's, he noted, and enormous swaths of sweat darkened her armpits behind the fattest, softest-looking upper arm he had ever seen.

"Your first time here, isn't it?"

"I'd like to see Billy Cobb."

"Billy'd like to see you, I'm sure." She winked, partially loosening her fake eyelash. Out shot one stubby-fingered hand. "Five dollars, Mr. Wilson."

"Five!"

She recoiled indignantly, her puffy, doughlike brow furrowing. "For your information, sir, you are standing in *the* finest house in the entire city."

"Okay, okay." Begrudgingly, he counted out five ones. She counted them twice, then held each one up in turn to the light of a hideous-looking, heavily tasseled reading lamp.

"For chrissakes, Emma, they're legit. I'm no damn counterfeiter!"

"Please! Kindly control your filthy mouth in my presence. I'll have you know my father was a minister."

And his daughter's a fat whore peddler, he thought, successfully resisting the urge to say so out loud.

Out came her hand a second time. "Give me your weapon." He started to protest. "House rules. You'll get it back when you leave." He complied resignedly. "Thank you. This way, Mr. Wilson."

She led him down a narrow hallway past an unnamed, scantily clad priestess holding a lighted flambeau. Pausing before a door, she knocked.

"Billy... Gentleman caller, dear."

"Ah'm busy, Emma, be done in two minutes."

Emma nodded and leered seductively at Raider, disclosing two gold teeth and a tongue half the size of a jelly doughnut, he thought, slightly revolted at the sight.

"Wait here, Mr. Wilson."

"For chris..."

"Tut, tut, tut. Language..."

Off she floated, leaving him standing at the door. He pressed his ear to it, but could hear nothing save the muffled squeaking of bedsprings. From another room came the sound of laughter. Overhead, from somewhere on the second floor, he could faintly hear a bottle shattering. Back in the front room somebody was playing the piano.

The door opened. An elderly man with a full white beard and monocle, and cheeks so red they were almost purple, came dragging out. In such woeful condition did he appear, Raider wondered if he'd make it to the street door without collapsing.

"Your turn, brother," he mumbled.

Raider grunted and went inside.

Billy was sitting at her vanity, fussing with her hair. She saw him in her mirror and swung about, instantaneously angry.

"You!"

Raider closed the door. "Don't start, goddamn it! Get peaceable. Just hear me out. Then, if you want, I'll leave."

She was staring at him, her features softening. "What in the world..."

His fingers sought his eye, carefully avoiding contact. "Accident."

"Who hit you? Come ovah heah."

She wet a cloth and began gently daubing his eye. He tensed and winced.

"Relax, don't be such a baby."

"Go easy, it hurts."

Her robe had gaped open, revealing one full, round, thoroughly delectable-looking breast, the nipple as firm and hard as a spike head.

He took hold of her wrist, gently lowering her hand.

"Billy..."

"What? You know, Ah oughta be callin' Lenny in heah and have y'all tossed out on youh eah. Ah'm mad as hell at y'all."

"I know, but you gotta at least let me explain." He held her wrists and her attention. "I want to level with you, Billy, I'm no western-gear salesman."

Tilting her head back, she laughed raucously. It took her fully thirty seconds before she got control of herself. "What do you take me foh, man? Ah may be a whoah, but ah'm no stupid whoah. Ah knew y'all wasn't no salesman. Look at y'all, foh mercy's sakes. Y'all got no pinky-finger diamond ring, no derby, no classy duds. Y'all sure 'nough ain't got the slick line o' jabber every other salesman evah come in heah got." She sobered. "What are you, John, detective?"

"Pinkerton."

"Ah knew it! Come to town to help get the goods on Mr. E. and his friends, right?"

"Right. To help Chief Hennessey."

"And wheah'd you get that lovely eye?"

"Chief Hennessey. We had what you might call a little difference of opinion."

"Aren't you two supposed to be on the same side?"

"Never mind 'bout that. Billy, I'm gonna trust you. If after I tell you what I'm 'bout to you go running to them and finger me..."

"Ah wouldn't do such a thing. What do y'all take me for!" He stared at her worriedly. "What's the matter?"

"It's the other way round. Me bringing you in might just finger you."

"Ah'm already in."

"I don't get you."

"That phony doctah, the blond fella, whoevah he was murdered Dulcie Mae got a good look at me. And Sister Elizabeth. He might not go aftah her on account o' her being a nun and all. Ah mean anybody's got to be crazy with the heat to murder a nun, don't you think? But me, ah'm fair game."

"You got a point, lady." He sighed. "You can blame me. I roped you in."

"Ah asked in, John." She paused. "That's not youh real name."

He hesitated and grinned. "It's Raider."

"That's a funny name."

He scowled. "No funnier than corn Cobb."

He explained why he and Doc had come to New Orleans, avoiding privileged information, specifics, realizing as he consciously reined his tongue against telling her more than what was necessary that he didn't actually know very much. Doc had the bulk of it, working shoulder to shoulder with Hennessey as he had been, talking George Provenzano into appearing as the prosecution's star witness.

Nevertheless, weighing the pros and cons of taking her into his confidence, he had to come down on the side of doing so—for a number of reasons. She was straight. She knew the town, the people, the bad people. She had already proven he could depend on her. She had already shown her eagerness to help; introducing him to Dulcie Mae; standing temporary guard outside her door, for all the good it did. Now she was listening, serious-eyed and attentive. Out of friendship toward him? Newfound bitterness toward *them* for what they had done to her best friend? Her reasons weren't important; all that really was was that he could count on her. He knew it, felt it. She hated Esposito, hated the mob, the disease infecting the city, holding it in fear and subjugation.

"What do you know 'bout the higher-ups?" he asked, "Esposito's buddies, his *compadres.*"

"Ah hear tell there's at least twenty. They have meetings all the time, what they call the Soo-preme Council."

"Where do they meet?"

"Ah don't know, but ah could maybe find out. They're business meetings, you know."

Raider clucked. "Got to decide whose blood gets spilled next. Didn't Dulcie Mae ever say where they met?"

"Nope. Could be in Mr. E's house on Chartres Street. It's the big brick one with the ivy round the front doah. Ah know something else—at the meetings they all weah black hoods with the eyes cut out."

"Halloween. That's where they no doubt plan the murders, hand out the jobs, suchlike."

"Y'all are getting a funny look in youh eye..."

"I'd purely love to be a fly on the wall at one o' those get-togethers, hoods or no. I bet they spill their guts out."

"Nobody gets in 'less they're one o' the higher-ups and s'posed to be theah."

"All the madams pay off, right?"

"Foh protection. Lenny, Emma's bouncer, his real name's Leonard Dibrozano, he's one of 'em."

"Figures."

They talked for about ten minutes. Raider raised a point, stressing it emphatically, one that Billy just as emphatically disagreed with. He proposed that after tonight they no longer see one another, definitely not in town.

"If you want to help . . ."

"Ah do!"

"Ssssh, keep it down. We'll have to meet someplace well away from Jackson Square. No more Bird Cage and not this place. You know the area, you pick a safe spot."

"What are y'all so 'fraid for? Ah'm not 'fraid o' them bastards. Ah owe them, John."

"Raider," he corrected.

"Ah like John better."

"It's not my name."

"It is to me. Was, and is."

"Have it your way."

She came to him, all lavender, softness, and warmth, placing her slender hands on his shoulders, slipping them around his neck. The loosely fashioned knot in the sash of her robe fell apart; the two folds opened. She was mother naked. He sighed inwardly. Her hands were hard against the nape of his neck, pushing his mouth down upon hers. Her quim was hard against his quiescent cock, gyrating slowly, grinding, working. He sighed aloud.

"What's the matter, love?"

"We got to talk," he said mildly, his tone slightly pleading.

"We already did. Time we got down to business. How 'bout I get y'all hard as a carpenter's slick and y'all stick it in me all the way up to the root."

He groaned. "I wish you wouldn't talk so . . ."

"Y'all know how to stop me."

She undressed him deftly, with a well-practiced hand, he noted glumly, quickly getting him down to the buff. Kneeling before him, lifting her lovely breasts upward to sandwich his cock, she began rubbing it, rubbing, setting it throbbing, rising, stiffening, pulsing, crimsoning, purpling . . . A carpenters's slick.

"God Almighty, woman . . ."

"What now?"

"You're gonna bust it into little pieces. You keep it up it'll explode, itty bitty chunks all over the damn room!"

She laughed, and laving her lips, ringed the head of his cock so lightly he could scarcely feel it. The wetness formed a cushion on which her burning lips glided up and down it. Up and down, up and down. Then she stopped, easing momentarily free, uttering sounds of pure enjoyment, of satisfaction and eagerness to press on.

Once more she took him in, riding her fiery mouth full length to his root, devouring him. He flinched, steeling himself, digging his nails into his palms, clamping his eyes so tight his eyeballs felt crushed, and came, splattering her throat with come. She swallowed greedily, her tongue whipping, washing his cock shining clean.

Quickly, she got him rigid again and, lying on the bed, spread her legs wide. He mounted her and she guided his head between her thighs, between her lips, slowly, exquisitely, filling the adit of her quim. He thrust forward, entering, scraping her clitoris erect and hard as a steel button. She squealed, driving her haunches upward, slamming her cunt hard against him, gyrating, driving, hammering, sledging . . . They came as one, Raider groaning, she crying out joyfully.

Raider left Billy's company an hour later with two things: his manhood as limp and exhausted as he had ever known it to be, and the understanding that he and Billy would meet again two days hence across the river in Gretna. He had asked her to find out where the Mafia's Supreme Council meetings were held. Esposito's house seemed the likely place, but he wanted to be absolutely certain where. And when the next one was scheduled for. He did not want to duplicate the efforts of the police, in particular Hennessey's personal undercover activities, but the fact that Billy lived and plied her trade in the very shadow of the mob, as it were, was too good an opportunity to let slip by unseized. She could not help but hear things, now that she planned to begin listening in earnest. She was bright, she was clever, she knew instinctively how to protect herself.

She could, he assured himself, be helpful. If she got lucky, extremely helpful.

He was mainly concerned with plotting the mob's upcoming moves. He also wanted to know how the twenty "nobles," Esposito's hierarchy, got along among themselves. There was always scrambling at the foot of any throne. Were there petty jealousies? Jealousies not so petty? Were there personality clashes and other conflicts? There had to be, he told himself. Wherever there was a group, whatever their purpose, there was always internal conflict. Somebody always had his eye on the other fellow's share. Somebody always had too much ambition and too little regard for cooperation. From all appearances, bloody though the decks may have been, Giuseppe Esposito ran a tight ship. Hopefully, Billy would be able to find out for him just how tight. Just how loose?

Emma greeted him outside with something less than enthusiasm.

"You sure as hell get your money's worth, cowboy," she said coldly.

"Tut, tut, tut. Language. Where's my hardware?"

Opening a wicker basket, she got out his gun and returned it. A third party was in the room, a young, good-looking man, blond hair, blue eyes. Glancing at him out of the corner of his eye as he holstered his Peacemaker, Raider got the impression that he was a college man. He had Doc's smooth edges, the unmistakable aura of refinement of the educated Easterner. Like Doc, he dressed tastefully and expensively. The centerpiece of his ensemble was a horseshoe no bigger than Raider's thumbnail studded with diamond chips. He was sitting at the piano, aimlessly exploring the scales with one finger. Emma turned to him, glowing.

"You can go in now, Mr. Masello."

The name surprised Raider. He looked anything—German, English, whatever—but Italian. As this skimmed across his mind, he recoiled at his prejudice. People should pigeonhole pigeons, not people. The man grinned at Emma, displaying fine, even teeth. Getting up from the bench, he started down the hallway.

What was a young, good-looking guy like that doing in a cathouse? wondered Raider. Walk him into the Bird Cage and he wouldn't get as far as the bar without every woman in the place falling all over him. Mentally shelving his curiosity, he thanked Emma and left.

He was tired and aching, his afflicted eye by now almost entirely closed. But this latest turn pleased him. And he was even more pleased that he hadn't left town. He could leave Hennessey, even leave Doc, but not Billy, not with her bitter as gall toward him over what had happened to Dulcie Mae.

What was he saying? He couldn't leave Doc. He'd never walked out on a case in his life. He'd never left anybody holding the satchel, much less his partner. It was past one in the morning. Mr. Flasharity would be back in the room fast asleep by now. He'd go back, wake him, and touch bases. He wondered fleetingly if Doc had been able to calm down Hennessey. His conscience told him to hope so.

He was passing the narrow, impenetrably dark alley alongside Emma Pickett's house when he heard an outcry.

"Billy!"

No mistake. Down the alley he tore, drawing his iron as he ran. He pulled up under her window, the only one showing a light inside. Holstering his gun, he grabbed the sill and pulled himself upward, speedily arousing all the aches and pains in his upper body. Over the sill he scrambled. Masello had Billy by a fistful of robe, the point of his knife pricking the soft flesh just under her chin. His glance shifted toward Raider, poised with one foot inside, one knee on the sill, his six-gun out again and aiming.

"Back off, you son of a bitch. I'll blow your head off. Let her go!"

Masello laughed, tightening his hold. In the next second he would swing her about, offering her back to block his line of fire, surmised Raider. But to his surprise Masello did not move her. Instead, he laughed again, releasing her robe. Digging in his jacket pocket, he held up his fist.

"Shoot, cowboy, go ahead!"

Raider muttered, taking dead aim at his head, a good seven inches above hers. Again Masello laughed. He opened his hand; out fell cartridges, tumbling to the floor. Raider froze, frowning, gaping at his gun in his hand.

"Son of a bitch . . ."

"Tut, tut, tut. Language. Stay where you are, I'll be done here in two shakes. You're next. Ha ha ha . . ."

Her attacker's attention concentrated on Raider, Billy took a wild chance. His knife continued poised, prepared to jab her throat, but he wasn't looking at her. She jerked her head to one side and clear, at the same time bringing her right leg up between his legs, driving her shin hard into his crotch. He yelled and doubled over. She wrenched free, casting about wildly.

"Under the bed!" boomed Raider.

Down on all fours, she scrambled under the bed. Knife in hand, Masello bent over, and slashed wildly, missing the back of her leg by a hair. Raider cursed and flung his empty gun at him. Masello ducked just in time. It clattered against the wall behind him. Straightening, he turned his full attention on Raider, his face twisted in a vicious leer.

"You want to be first? You got it." He gestured, waggling him closer with his fingers. "Come on, come on."

Raider got out Esposito's knife, flicking it open, holding it upright, the blade catching the lamplight. Masello started, blinking, scowling.

"Surprise! You come on, pretty boy."

They began circling slowly, stalking each other, occasionally slashing the air, testing lunges, pulling free of danger.

He knew how to handle a knife, reflected Raider ruefully. He could probably pick a wing off a fly in midair.

"What are you waiting for, cowboy? Let's see how good you are."

"Good enough to take this offa your big boss. Come on, try me."

Masello lunged, his blade flashing upward, the tip catching Raider inside his outstretched arm, grazing his wrist lightly, drawing crimson. Billy's eyes peered out from under the bed. She gasped.

"Keep under there, damn it!" roared Raider irritably.

"That was close," said Masello. "Next one'll be it. Don't worry, it doesn't hurt much. Feels hot, so they tell me. I wouldn't know, I've never had the experience. Then comes the cut. Ear to ear. You're going to look good in red. It's your color. I've going to paint this whole room with you, everything but the ceiling. With both of you. Ha ha, ha—you're going to be my paintbrushes."

They continued circling, dueling, blades occasionally clicking. He was strong, sensed Raider, with a powerful wrist and forearm. He handled a knife expertly, with remarkable dexterity, as if it were a natural extension of his hand. And, despite his size, he was as light on his feet as a panther. He groaned inwardly. He himself was moving like a gluttonous grizzly, his legs become leaden with weariness; his arm, his ability to thrust and react slowing; his upper body aches and pains signaling their whereabouts, throbbing reminders of Hennessey's resentment. His one fully opened working eye followed Masello circling. He watched him kick the vanity bench backwards into the corner. He lunged. Raider stepped aside, at the same time sucking in his gut. The blade shot by him, just barely missing. He stepped forward, driving his own knife hard upware, missing cleanly, Masello jackknifing out of the way, whirling on his heel, coming back at him.

It was like dueling two people, he reflected, so fast did his opponent move, so skillfully, so perfectly balanced. What little energy Raider had remaining was rapidly draining away—while Masello appeared as fresh as morning.

He was enjoying this; his face betrayed it. He relished the test, inwardly gloating, confident that he was the better man, certain beyond doubt that he would win. He was beginning to toy with him, thought Raider resentfully, suddenly despising the murdering pig.

One thing he fixed in mind: He must stay in the center of the room, well away from the corners and the narrow-space side of the bed. If Masello got him into a corner or on the other side of the bed it would be all over.

They stood with their scowls inches apart, upper bodies bent slightly forward, knives low, blades angled upward. Masello faked a lunge, shifting his shoulders, suckering Raider into committing himself, moving too far forward and up on his toes in retaliation, losing his balance for a split second. He regained it just in time to avoid a thrust straight into his belly. The point of Masello's blade clicked against his belt buckle.

"Close, cowboy, too close. Had enough yet? How about it, shall we wind it up. What do you say?"

"Keep talking, you murdering bastard."

His good eye stinging from sweat salt, he blinked rapidly to clear it. And attacked, again missing cleanly. Masello countered, Raider slipping sideways, tangling his feet, falling, com-

ing down on the bed. His face masked with triumph, Masello
dove for him. But anticipating this, Raider had already started
his roll, avoiding the thrust, reaching for the floor at the end
of the bed with his free left hand to break his fall. Pain shot
through his wrist like a hot wire as he landed.

"Goddamn!"

Up on his feet, the wall at his back, he faced his attacker.
Masello was out of position on the far side of the bed, out of
reach, forced to come around the corner to get at him. He
started for him. This was it, thought Raider grimly. Positioned
as he was, the wall behind him, the vanity table to his left, all
he could do would be to jump up on the bed. But Masello was
left-handed; if he tried to get out that way he'd catch him in
the gut before his feet hit, the easiest and surest possible move.

Masello had started around the corner. Suddenly, his face
went blank as he stumbled and fell, pitching forward laterally,
three feet in front of Raider. Down he went, his free hand
flying out to catch the edge of the vanity table, his upraised
knife in the other jabbing him full in the stomach. He screamed,
arched his back, straightened, lay still. Billy emerged from
under the bed.

"He fell . . ." began Raider mystified.

"Ah tripped him, you dummy. Got him by the ankle!"

"You saved my bacon. I was a goner for sure."

"He sure knew how to handle a knife. Is he dead?"

"He can't get any deader."

A loud pounding punished the door. Billy adjusted her robe,
knotting the sash and unlocking the door. In stormed Emma
Picket followed by a burly, bald-headed man with a patch over
one eye and a white scar running straight down from it, bi-
secting his cheek and hooking under his chin. Lenny, mused
Raider.

"What the devil . . ." began Emma. She stared at the dead
man and glared at Raider.

"Don't start up with me, you fat slob," he hissed. "You
emptied my gun. You set me up."

"You're a bald-faced liar!"

Lenny glowered and took a step forward. Up came Raider's
knife. Emma's hand across his belly stopped him.

"Get that ape outta here, 'fore I slice his ugly face off his
goddamn head!"

Emma nodded to Lenny. He started to say something, changed his mind, and withdrew.

"Emma," said Raider menacingly, shaking one finger under her heavily powdered, slightly misshapen nose. "Listen good. Don't talk, just listen. You set Billy up, you set me up. I'm gonna return the favor. I'm gonna have the law close this dump up tighter than a rivet in a rail."

"You listen to me, Mr. Whatever-your-real-name-is. I didn't mean any harm to anybody, least of all her. It was Masello. You don't understand. Everybody in business in this town has to do as they say. Or else."

"I know that. You think I'm stupid? Only when he showed up he didn't know I was in here. So how would he know I checked my gun out front, if you didn't tell him?"

"I didn't have to tell him you were carrying a gun. He followed you in."

"That's a damn lie!"

"It's the almighty truth!"

"It could be, John," interposed Billy.

"All right, all right. But you let him in here without batting an eye to cut her up, to kill her just like he killed her girl friend."

"What could I do? We do what we're told, every mother's child."

"Even to helping with cold-blooded murder?"

"Even to that." She turned apologetic eyes on Billy. "I am sorry, Billy, and ashamed. I wouldn't hurt you for the world. You know that, dear heart. You're like my own flesh and blood..."

"All I know is what happened. Ah'm getting outta this hole."

"You wouldn't desert me!"

Billy gaped, unable to believe her ears. "Are y'all funning me?"

"All right, leave. If you feel you have to. If that's your heart's desire."

"Heart and every othah part o' me. Ah got to get outta this town. It's getting too damn dangerous for a working girl. Ah'll send somebody round for mah trunk in the morning."

"Whatever you say, dear heart."

"Y'all owe me fohty-six bucks."

"You'll get it. I run an honest house. You know that, Billy."

"Honest. Noisy. Bloody. See you keep that overgrown lummox 'way from me. He'd purely love to finish what that one on the floah started. Mr. E.'d love that. Get out, Emma, ah'm sick o' the sight o' you!"

Emma looked properly hurt, and glanced at Raider questioningly.

"He stays," said Billy. "He's the only protection I got."

Emma withdrew. The instant she was out the door Raider began delivering himself of some well-chosen opinions.

"Some protection you got from me! I oughta be lying there dead instead o' him, and you too, for me being so damn dumb! Stupid as an ore-cart jack-mule!"

"What?"

He hauled out his Peacemaker. "I took this back and never even checked the chambers. Not a look! Just thank you, ma'am, tip o' the brim, and good night." He broke the gun, revealing the six empty eyes. "I'm supposed to be professional, you know, think on my feet, know all the tricks, Mr. Cagey, Mr. Smart. Some smart!" He was suddenly blistering. "DAMN!" He slammed his fist into the wall, howled, and pulled it back, shaking it vigorously.

Ten minutes later they were hurrying down John Street in the direction of the Hotel Gregg. Billy was counting her money.

"This isn't fohty-six dollahs, it's fifty even. She made a mistake."

"No mistake. That's four bucks worth o' her conscience."

The streets were deserted. Her heels clicked loudly against the pavement. From somewhere nearby came the sound of a Victrola playing classical music. The stars were out, and the moon bathed the city in a grayish-blue glow.

"John . . ."

"What?"

"Y'all think Lenny'll take it out on her?"

"Take what? She didn't do anything, except follow Masello's orders. Damn, I wish he hadn't bought it. I coulda hauled him in, had him patched up, locked up, and sweat a barrel and a half o' goodies outta him."

"He'd nevah talk. None o' the small fry do. It'd be committing suicide."

"He'd be committing it if he didn't, the murdering son of

a bitch. I shoulda cut his heart out and give it to the cats in the alley."

One shoe came off; she limped along three steps. "Slow down, can't y'all?"

He glanced back at her and laughed. Her peacock feather straw hat was comically askew, her eye makeup was running down both cheeks, her lipstick, hastily reapplied as she was leaving, appeared to be massing at the corner of her mouth, her dress was on crooked...

"What the hell's so funny?"

"You."

She swung her bag. He cringed, taking the blow lightly, and laughed again. She got her shoe back on, muttering vilely as she did so. Again they started off.

CHAPTER EIGHT

Doc sat up in bed, bleary-eyed, rubbing his eyes with the heels of his hands like a small boy and pouting indignantly.

"What time is it?"

"Night time," replied Raider, winking at Billy seated on the opposite side of the bed. "What's happening with Hennessey?"

"What do you think? The man's on fire he's so mad. Rade, there's a limit to how personal you can get. You called him a son of an Irish bitch!"

"It just slipped out. I meant to say Irish son of a bitch."

"It's the same thing!"

"I guess. Still, couldn't he let bygones be bygones? Couldn't you calm him down?"

"Can you calm down a Kansas twister with kind words?" He yawned. "He'll get over it. He's got bigger things to think about than loud-mouthed plowboys with chips on their shoulders and deep-seated guilt feelings."

"What guilt? I got no guilt!"

"Ah think he's talking 'bout Dulcie Mae, John."

"Exactly, 'John.'"

Seeing it was two against one on a subject much too painful to pursue, Raider changed it.

"Doc, this idea o' us splitting up and meeting at outta-the-way spots all over town doesn't make sense. Not anymore. Esposito and his crew know we're a team. They got eyes all over. Makes no difference whether we're apart or together."

"Hand me a smoke out of my pocket there, will you?"

Raider obliged him. Doc lit up.

"You're probably right," he said. "Everything's changed so in a matter of hours. We got lucky with the fruit man, thank the Lord. Cross your fingers they don't find him."

"Don't bet on that. Don't bet on beans. What's the next move?"

"I don't know what yours is. Mine's to get some sleep. We'll discuss it in the morning."

Billy stood up and began undressing.

"What do you think you're doing?" asked Raider.

"What does it look like? Ah'm so tired ah can't keep my eyes open."

"Be a gentleman, Raider," said Doc. "Make believe you are. Offer the lady a place to sleep."

Raider bristled. "Where am I supposed to?"

Billy leered. "You'h welcome on eitheh side o' me."

"Not 'nough room."

"How 'bout on top?" She winked slowly, suggestively. Doc laughed; Raider flushed. He snapped his fingers.

"I got it. We pull both beds together and you can sleep half on his, half on mine. How 'bout that?"

"Perfect," said Billy.

Doc grunted and rolled over on his face. Raider aligned both beds in juxtaposition and undressed down to his skivvies. Billy blithely, and without a trace of self-consciousness, removed every stitch she had on, then lay down on the line joining the two beds, snuggling close to Doc. He was back to sleep, breathing lightly, smiling blissfully.

"There's plenty o' room," observed Raider sourly. "You don't have to get that close to him."

"What's the matter, jealous?"

"He's asleep, what's to be jealous? Hey, would you mind

covering up? Don't you have no shame?" She pulled Doc's
sheet loose, partially covering her nudity, then closed Raider's
top sheet over Doc's.

"Will that do you?"

Raider blew out the lamp and got into bed, his shoulder
touching hers, igniting a light and pleasant tingling sensation.
Reaching over, she took hold of his manhood and began gently
massaging him.

"Anytime you'h ready, John."

He grunted, removed her hand, and rolled over on his side.
She too rolled over, pushing her breasts up against his back
and her quim hard against his buttocks.

"Anytime, John."

She waited. He was asleep, or pretending to be. She smiled
in the darkness. Give him twenty minutes, she thought, reaching over and taking hold of his cock once more.

Raider could be grateful for one thing: If Hennessey held
any brief against him for the mix-up the night before, he was
certainly making a praise-worthy effort to hide his feelings.
The two Pinkertons had taken Billy Cobb to breakfast, picked
up her belongings at 25 John Street, and put her in a hansom
bound for Gretna across the river. There she would be safe,
Doc persisted in assuring Raider. Raider fervently hoped so.

Neither mentioned Billy to Hennessey, sitting in his office
later that morning. The chief was in a particularly buoyant
mood, well rested, sharp in conversation, giving all outward
appearance of inward optimism over the latest turn in his cru-
sade to rid New Orleans of the Mafia. Eyeing and listening to
him, Doc found his good mood contagious. Not so Raider.
Whether his partner was displaying his customary reserve and
effecting his customary scowl because of what had happened
in the hallway the previous night or whether he was worried
over George Provenzano's safety as well as Billy's, Doc could
only surmise. But whenever Hennessey asked Raider a question
the answer came back a monosyllable, a grunt, or merely a
nod.

"I've got a meeting with Mayor Shakespeare at noon sharp,"
said Hennessey. "It's going to be nice to be able to bring him
some good news for a change."

"What good news is that?" Raider asked, suddenly waxing

what was for him downright garrulous, thought Doc.

"Provenzano, of course."

"He still alive?"

"Rade . . ."

"You're in a happy mood this morning." Hennessey grinned good-naturedly. "How's the eye?"

"Sore. How's your hand?"

"Gentlemen, gentlemen," interrupted Doc, fearful that the next question out of Raider would have some reference to Hennessey's Irish mother. "Can't we forget about last night?"

"I can if you can," said the chief, extending his hand to Raider.

Raider eyed it.

"Rade . . ." began Doc threateningly.

They shook hands. The door opened. Frank Montaigne stuck his head in.

"Morning, fellows. You wanted to see me, Dave?"

Hennessey held up a letter by the corner of the envelope. He beamed. "Congratulations, Frank."

Montaigne's eyes started from his head. Snatching the letter from him, he ripped it open and read it.

"Lieutenant," added Hennessey.

"Congratulations," said Doc.

"Yeah," said Raider.

"Oh boy. Oh boy, oh boy, oh boy," muttered Montaigne. "Give me ten minutes, Dave. I'm going home and tell Paulette. She's going to do cahtwheels! I may myself!"

"Take fifteen."

Montaigne was gone, running, practically dancing down the hallway out of sight. Hennessey got up and began aimlessly examining the few shards of glass still remaining in the door.

"I may be sticking my neck out ten feet," he said solemnly, "but I'd be willing to bet a month's salary we'll be able to save the Mardi Gras." He turned to face them. "We can go before the grand jury in a week. I was up half the night going over Provenzano's files." He indicated a bulky manila envelope on the desk. "Between his records there and what he told us last night we can destroy the mob." He rubbed his hands together gleefully. "Three years work, nothing but one blank wall after the other. Now it's suddenly all rainbows! Beautiful! You don't know what this means to me. I'll tell you exactly. It means getting back this town. They kidnapped it, held it for ransom, and every decent man, woman, and child has had to pay and pay and pay. Now we've got 'em. I don't believe it. I've got to pinch myself!

"I can't wait for the trial. I'll be on pins and needles. This'll be the longest week of my life." He paused, crossing to where Doc was sitting. He laid a huge hand on his shoulder. "And I've got you to thank for it, Doc. Oh, and you too, Raider."

"Mmmm."

"I had Peter Provenzano and lost him. And couldn't touch the other two. They'd see me coming, they'd run the other way. I never had two words with either George or Joe after he was killed. But you got to George. Now he's ours. Listen to me, I want both of you to come with me to this meeting with the mayor. I want to introduce you. After all, it was his idea we send up to Chicago for help. How about it, boys?"

"I don't know, Dave," said Doc. "After all, it's your show."

"We don't want to crab your act," ventured Raider.

"I'm asking you to come, inviting you. We'll be having lunch at his house. What's two more places at the table, eh? Hey, if I tell him I asked you and you turned me down, he'll snap my head off. You're coming. That's all there is to it." He raised his fist and shook it victoriously. "What a day! What a life! Beautiful, just beautiful!"

CHAPTER NINE

Mayor Joseph Shakespeare bore a remote resemblance to President Rutherford B. Hayes, decided Doc, upon being introduced to His Honor by Chief Hennessey. The mayor, like the President, chose to drape the lower half of his lean face with mustache and full beard, but unlike Hayes's white and somewhat scraggly hirsuteness, Shakespeare's was coal black all the way up to his temples. He was balding in front and combed his straight hair to the left across his scalp. His eyes, like the President's, were hazel and searching; he appeared to "listen" with them.

His residence was furnished with gaudy magnificence, a profusion of velvet, plush, and damask, gilt and plate glass. The five of them—the company included District Attorney Charles J. Luzenberg—sat at lunch, enjoying crayfish salad and sipping a somewhat indifferent Chablis, Doc confided to Raider without words, grimacing slightly as he sampled it, and complimenting it too heartily when Shakespeare asked if he liked it. Luzenberg appeared as pessimistic as the mayor was optimistic over the state of things, persistently decrying what he described as the tenuousness of the state's case against the Mafia.

"I don't see as we're any better off now than we were last week or last month," he observed in a whining tone. "I don't trust this Provenzano. How do we know he just doesn't have a grudge against Esposito and the Matrangas?"

"He most assuredly does," said Shakespeare expansively.

"But if he's concocted a whole mess of cock and bull just to get even with them, we're so heavily dependent upon the man, his facts, his testimony, the entire case could cave in. You can bet your boots they're going to line up the best legal representation money can buy. They'll be coming into this thing fighting for their lives."

Shakespeare winked at Doc. "Afraid you won't be able to slug it out with their boys, is that it, Charlie? Getting antsy?" He clapped him on the shoulder good-naturedly. "You're beginning to sound like a bride a week away from 'I do.'" He laughed.

Luzenberg snorted and scowled. He was small, birdlike, oddly handsome: deep-set blue eyes, neatly combed blond hair, classic nose and mouth. But somehow, thought Doc, studying him over a forkful of crayfish, they didn't combine very well. Perhaps it was his nose that threw everything off. Perhaps it was a bit too large for the setting. He was a whiner, the sort Raider might describe as getting eyestrain searching for rain clouds in a beautiful blue sky.

"I'm being the devil's advocate, that's all. Call me a pessimist."

"You're a pessimist," said Raider, snickering.

The mayor roared. Then his smile gave way to a serious look. "The man's right about one thing: They'll have the sharpest, cleverest lawyers in Dixie."

"Which is why we're collecting the solidest evidence we can," said Hennessey, nodding determinedly at Luzenberg, as if to punctuate this assertion.

"It obviously hinges on George Provenzano," said Doc. "If we can keep him healthy, keep his bitterness level high and his courage just as high you'll be in good shape, Counselor."

Luzenberg shrugged. "There are going to have to be other

witnesses. We can hardly go to trial with one man in a case like this."

"There'll be other witnesses," said Hennessey. "Mostly small fry, but they'll corroborate what he says."

Luzenberg sipped his coffee and studied the chief down his nose. "Don't bet your life. I'm from Missouri. Experience warns me to be skeptical. Witnesses change their stories; they disappear; they can be bought and sold like cattle. It's a fact of life in cases like this. People hide their fears, even dismiss them, right up to the witness box. Then, all of a sudden, it's cold feet and second thoughts. When you're sitting in that chair under the judge, looking across at people like the Matrangas, Esposito, Bagnetto. When you see them looking back at you it's enough to change anybody's mind."

Hennessey picked up the manila envelope leaning against the leg of his chair. "You've seen these records, gentlemen." He held up a sheaf of papers. "This is your case, Counselor. Provenzano's verbal testimony is only the backup. This is what's going to make or break us. Make us, I say. Names, places, dates, the criminal history of the waterfront over the past two years."

"That envelope is dynamite, David," observed Shakespeare. "Where are you keeping it?"

"Last night locked in the safe in my office, but I know an even better place."

Luzenberg extended his hand. "Give it here, I'll take care of it."

"Not yet." Hennessey looked to the mayor for support. "When I finish pulling everything we've got together, then you'll get it all."

"It's all his digging," said Shakespeare. "We best let him handle it his way. Where you going to stash it, David?"

"With all due respect, Your Honor, I'd prefer not to say. Not that all of us here don't trust one another, but . . ."

Shakespeare grinned. "Whatever you say, son. It's your baby. Gentlemen, who's for a Cuban cigar? Just arrived, Miguel Panatellas, my favorite. And a spot of brandy to settle the fish."

Doc accepted both offers. Raider declined with his customary tactfulness.

"Not me. Cigars make me sick, and I can't stand woman's liquor. Too damn sweet."

Leaving the mayor's house, they parted company with Hennessey and Luzenberg and headed back to their hotel. It was a lovely day, the sky Delft-blue and cloudless, the sun golden and comfortably warm. At Doc's suggestion, they walked. Raider's aches were healing—all but his hand, which had been slightly injured in the attack on the wall of Billy Cobb's room. His knuckles were badly bruised. He kept flexing his fingers, Doc noticed.

"That D.A. dumps on just 'bout everything," Raider observed morosely.

"He's a lawyer. Cynicism is his stock in trade. Job's comforter. If he was all up and eager, chomping at the bit to get this thing into court, if he loses he looks foolish. If he goes into it complaining, fretting over his evidence and wins, it makes him look like a mastermind."

"You got it all figured."

"It's true, Rade. It's a game lawyers play. Everybody plays games. Make anything challenging you attempt look difficult, impossible, then when you solve the problem, save the life, win the case you look like a miracle worker."

"He's right 'bout one thing: Witnesses sure do knuckle under when the heat's turned on."

"Maybe not this time, Rade. This town is fed up with the Mafia. People have had all they can take. If the case does collapse in court, which I don't think will happen, I wouldn't be surprised if the man in the street takes matters into his own hands."

"Vigilantes? You and me gotta be long gone outta here if that happens. The last place I want to be when all hell busts loose is in the damn middle."

They reached the Hotel Gregg. Sitting in the lobby waiting for them, peacock feather straw hat, smile, and all was Billy Cobb. Raider swore.

"What in hell you doing back here?"

"Rade, keep it down, people are looking."

"Let 'em look! Billy . . ."

She turned to Doc. "How's that foh a welcome? Isn' he sweet? Isn' he gracious?"

"Have you found out something?" Doc asked, lowering his voice.

She nodded. Raider cast about anxiously. None of the occupants of the overstuffed chairs was paying the slightest attention to them.

"Let's get on up to the room," he said.

"No." Doc stayed him, his hand on his arm. "Let's go for a walk."

Outside on the sidewalk Doc headed them in the direction of Jackson Square.

"What's up, Billy?" Raider asked. "And before you say, when you get done we'll have a drink or something and put you in a cab and back you go, understand?"

"Doc, will y'all kindly tell youh friend Ah'm old enough to take care o' myself? Ah been doing it since Ah was 'leven. Ah don't need a daddy."

"What you need is a slat 'cross the backside," snapped Raider. "Can't you get it through your head this game's for keeps? I woulda thought last night would tell you how serious, how dangerous—"

"Rade, Rade," interrupted Doc. "Will you let her talk?"

Raider deliberately avoided her eyes, signaling permission granted.

"John," said Billy, "recollect y'all asked about the Supreme Council meeting?"

"What, may I ask, would that be?" Doc asked.

Billy and Raider explained in brief.

"Theah's a meeting tonight," she whispered, her tone conspiratorial. "Ten o'clock."

Raider stopped walking. "Who says? How do you know?"

"Ah got it from a friend of a friend—reliable. It's true, it is."

"What did you do, get outta that cab over to Gretna and walk round buttonholing folks?"

"Rade, will you stop needling? Billy, where is this meeting?"

"Mr. E.'s house on Chartres Street. Theah's this big meeting room in the cellah."

"Oh boy," said Raider, licking his lips. "We got to get up a raid. Bust in with twenty guns, fifty, and clean house!"

"No, no, no. That's ridiculous. What would it get us? What

good would it do Hennessey? They have a right to meet. In a private house? Every right in the world. Isn't it more important we find out what goes on? Why they're meeting? What they're up to?"

"How you figure to do that, hide in somebody's pocket?"

"I don't know how. My point is there's nothing to be gained by a raid. So we bring them in. Then what? What do we hold them on?"

"Unlawful assembly."

"That's an assumption, Rade."

"What do you think they'll be up to, swapping dirty stories? Selling each other lottery tickets? What?"

Doc addressed Billy. "You understand what his trouble is, don't you? He can't stand being wrong. God forbid he ever has to admit it. And he hasn't the remotest concept of how the law works. Any law. Just blunder in and break every head in sight."

"Why don't you shut your damn big mouth, Mr. Flasharity!"

"Let's get something straight, Rade . . ."

"Quiet, both o' you!" She stood hands on hips, glaring at first one, then the other. "All you two do is bicker, bicker, bicker! Ah'm sorry Ah told y'all, sorry Ah come all the way back . . ."

"Now, now, now," said Doc soothingly. "Pay no attention to us. Force of habit. We're very grateful, Billy, I can't tell you how grateful. This could be very helpful if we can only figure how to use it. Actually, Rade, I think we ought to get together with Dave. He should be the one to make a decision."

"What decision might that be?"

"He might decide to stage a raid."

"I thought you just said there's nothing to be gained by a raid? Didn't he just say that, Billy, didn't he? I heard him!"

"I know what I said. What I'm trying to say now is that he, the chief, should be apprised."

"Screw that. I say we tell him. Let's get on over there."

CHAPTER TEN

Chief Hennessey was not at the station when the Pinkertons arrived with Billy. Sergeant, now Lieutenant Montaigne, did not know where he was. He had come in fifteen minutes before "to pick something up," and left. Raider and Doc told Montaigne about the meeting scheduled for that night, but he was in as deep a quandary as were they as to how to utilize the information. He promised to tell Hennessey if and when the chief came back, and they left. They bought Billy an étouffée and café brûlot in a restaurant down the street from the station, then put her into a cab and sent her back to Gretna.

They waited all afternoon for Hennessey to return, but he failed to. At 5:30 they left. At eight o'clock, following dinner, they were in the room when a knock sounded at the door. It was a uniformed officer, a sallow-looking wraith of a man standing behind an absurdly large mustache. He saluted.

"Officer Caselli. Lieutenant Montaigne sent me over. Something's happened he wanted you to know about right away."

"Happened?" asked Doc stiffening.

"The chief. He's been shot."

Doc gasped. Raider, who had been at the mirror shaving, came striding over.

"Is he . . ."

Caselli nodded.

"Good God," whispered Doc. "What happened?"

"He was ambushed. He stopped by the station about an hour ago. And left again. The lieutenant thinks he was heading home. He doesn't really know because they didn't get a chance to talk. The chief lives on Girod Street between Basin and Franklin."

"He was alone?" Doc asked. He was leaning against the jamb for support, his cheeks conspicuously chalky.

Caselli shook his head. "Captain O'Connor was with him. He's retired. He works now for the Boylan Protective Police. It's private. He told the lieutenant what happened."

"What did?" Raider asked, toweling his face.

"The captain left the chief at Rampart and Girod. He was walking down the block when he heard a shotgun, two blasts, then four pistol shots. He ran back and found the chief sitting on a stoop. He was bleeding something fierce. He said, 'They got me, Bill, but I gave them the best I could.' The captain looked down the street and saw a fellow walking fast, the only one in sight. He chased him for five blocks. He caught him. Captain O'Connor's in good shape."

"He brought him in?" Doc asked.

Caselli nodded. "He's locked up. The lieutenant's been questioning him."

"Let's go, Rade."

"Can't I at least get my damn shirt on!" burst out Raider petulantly.

"Move!"

The man Captain O'Connor had apprehended was a well-built, swarthy Italian who spoke broken English. He was, surprisingly, clean-shaven and smelled strongly of cologne. He also had a manicure, noted Doc.

Montaigne let the two Pinkertons into his cell. The lieutenant was badly shaken. He appeared to be in mild shock, shaking his head repeatedly and muttering to himself.

"Good luck, boys," he murmured, closing the cell door

behind them. "Maybe you can get something out of the bastahd."

"I never shoot nobody, I swear to God in heaven! I'ma *innocente!*"

"Shut up!" snapped Raider. He grabbed him by the shirtfront. "You listen to me, you piece o' garbage..."

"Rade, leave him alone. Let's not go off half-cocked."

"Murdering son of a bitch!"

"I no shoot nobody. My hands are clean. I'ma good citizen. I was a altar boy seven years. My mother wanted me to be a priest!"

"Shut up!"

"Keep it down, Rade, you don't have to perform for the rank and file." He lit a cheroot, blowing the smoke out lightly, and confronted the prisoner. "What's your name?"

"Enzo Carlone. I am a poor shoemaker. I have a wife and five children."

"How 'bout ten?" Raider asked. "Ten'll make us feel twice as sorry for you."

"Rade," muttered Doc exasperatedly. "Enzo, listen to me. You say you're innocent, I believe you." The abject fear began dissolving from the man's face. "But you were the only one in sight..."

"There were two others. I try to tell the cop. They both had guns. I saw. *They* shot him!" He mimed the action.

"You were just along for the show, right?" Raider looked at him witheringly.

"I'ma no kill him! I'ma no kill nobody!"

"But you know who did," said Doc. "What are their names?"

"I...I can't tell you. They would kill me!"

The dread returned, filling his eyes. He slowly drew his finger across his throat.

"Nobody's going to kill you," said Doc reassuringly. "You're safe as a baby in here."

"In here, anyplace, they kill me! Even talkin'a to you like this I am a dead man!"

He steadfastly refused to tell them anything. He hadn't seen any envelope, suddenly didn't know either of the men he claimed had done the actual shooting. He was merely walking along, minding his own business. Doc finally gave it up. The guard let them out. They stopped by Montaigne's office. He was still badly shaken. He shut his door and threw the bolt.

"I didn't even see Dave when he came in the second time. He was in and out."

"Where's Captain O'Connor?"

"He went with the boys to the morgue. He'll be coming back heah."

"Why did Dave come back twice, I wonder?" mused Doc aloud.

"I don't know why the first time, but the second must have been to pick up the envelope."

"The stuff Provenzano gave him?" Doc asked.

Montaigne nodded. "I went into his office aftah he left. I didn't know he'd gone. The door to the safe was left open. Right away I got suspicious. It's nevah left open. I looked inside. It was empty. So I figured he'd taken the envelope, right? I had seen him put it in when he came back from lunch at the mayor's." Montaigne paused and snapped his fingers. "That's right."

"What?" Doc asked.

"He mentioned then, when he stuck it in the safe, that he was going to take it home with him."

Doc nodded. "Only he never reached home. And when O'Connor brought in friend Enzo he didn't have the envelope on him."

Montaigne shook his head. "To tell you the truth, I nevah even thought about it, what with Dave and all. You can't imagine. When Bill told me I got sick to my stomach. I got dizzy. It felt like my whole body was going to explode."

"Nerves," said Doc solicitously.

"What a rotten thing to happen! They tried and tried to get him. They finally did, the bastahds!"

"That envelope was the whole case, Doc," said Raider dejectedly.

"I know. But how could they even know about it?"

"What don't they know? You can bet they got it. It sure isn't lying in the gutter back there. I mean if O'Connor saw it, he would have picked it up, wouldn't he?"

"That's right," said Montaigne.

"Which tells us something," said Doc. "Not much, but something. Enzo could be telling the truth about 'two other guys.' No murder weapon or weapons, no envelope. Maybe he was just along for the company."

Again Montaigne snapped his fingers. "I almost fohgot..." Reaching under his desk, he brought out a small, expensive-looking-satchel. The two top latches showed keyholes. "Enzo was carrying this when O'Connor caught up with him. We couldn't find the key when we searched him."

"He probably swallowed it," said Raider.

"You think the envelope's in heah?" asked Montaigne, wide-eyeing the satchel.

"Let's force the locks," said Doc, "and cross our fingers."

Montaigne got a screwdriver out of a desk drawer. Working patiently, he forced open one latch. He was working on the other one when a knock came at the door. Doc opened it to a well-built man in his late fifties wearing a face as Irish as Hennessey's, with a stogie stuck in it. At sight of the stogie, Raider grimaced. Montaigne introduced Captain O'Connor, then returned his attention to the latch.

"Stupid question," said Doc to the captain. "By chance did you see anybody else running away?"

"There was nobody else on the street."

"He was shot from ambush," said Raider.

O'Connor shrugged. "I figure he had to be. I didn't see. I was around the corner."

"Two shotgun blasts and four pistol shots," said Doc.

O'Connor nodded. "The pistol had to be Hennessey's. When I came running up he was sitting holding it. The first thing he said was 'I gave them the best I could.'"

"*Them*," said Doc.

"That doesn't mean beans, Doc," said Raider. "If he was bushwhacked he wouldn't be able to see how many were shooting. Two shots..."

"It could have been a double-barreled shotgun," said Doc.

"Could have been," said O'Connor. "I didn't see any weapon, except Dave's pistol. What does the prisoner say?"

"Not much," said Doc.

"You're going to have to really sweat the bastard," murmured O'Connor.

"I doubt if we'd get anything out of him. He's too afraid."

"Either that or making out like he is," said Raider.

Montaigne got the satchel unlocked. Setting it on his desk, he opened it. There was no envelope, no sawed-off shotgun, only a knife similar to the one Raider had taken from Esposito. There were also two curious-looking articles of clothing: a black silk cloak and hood.

"Halloween," muttered Raider, then immediately brightened. "Jesus Christ, the Supreme Council!" He snatched the hood and cloak from Montaigne, holding them up. "This is the uniform. When Billy first told me I recollect saying Halloween—kidding, you know. This is the Supreme Council. That son of a bitch back there is no more shoemaker than I am!"

"He's the first one I've evah seen with a manicure," observed Montaigne.

"He's one o' the big boys. The Supreme Council is all the big boys, twenty o' them." He glanced at the clock on the wall above the desk. It showed twenty-five past nine. "The meeting starts in thirty-five minutes. In Esposito's house in Chartres Street."

"Enzo was probably on his way there," observed O'Connor. "Come on, let's start steaming him. Let's bust a few fingers!"

Doc shook his head emphatically. "That won't do any good."

"The hell with him," said Raider. "I'm getting an idea, Doc. Listen, follow me. He's on his way to the meeting, but he starts out hanging round outside, waiting for Hennessey to leave so he can follow him. He's alone or maybe with another guy, maybe even two. They follow him to—"

"Basin Street," said O'Connor. "That's where I found him sitting on the stoop."

"They shoot him, grab the envelope, and run," continued Raider.

"You keep saying *they*," said Montaigne. "The captain heah only saw Enzo. No murdah weapon, no envelope."

"There *had* to be somebody with Enzo," said Doc. "If he was alone, he would have had time to toss the shotgun down a sewer, but he never would have disposed of the envelope. He was committing murder to get his hands on it. He'd hardly throw it away. Somebody must have been with him, and *that somebody's got the envelope.*"

"Let me finish, goddamn it!" snapped Raider. Again he held up the hood and cloak. "Enzo's on his way to the meeting. They kill Hennessey, then what did they do? What would you do if you and another guy gunned somebody down in the street in broad daylight?"

"Scatter," said O'Connor.

"Right. Which means whoever was with Enzo ran off in another direction, not knowing or caring which way he ran. *And couldn't know he got caught, right?* I mean the other fella's got the envelope, he's making tracks. It's every man for himself."

"What are you getting at, Rade?" Doc asked, rolling his eyes impatiently.

"Let me finish, you'll find out. If nobody knows Enzo got caught, and they most likely don't, then they'll be expecting him to show at the big meeting. They'll all be wearing hoods." He tossed the cloak on the desk and put on the hood. "Including me, Enzo."

"Are you crazy?" burst out Doc. "You actually think you can sneak into their meeting?"

"They'll find you out befoah you can take a deep breath," said Montaigne. "You don't speak Italian, you don't know what to do, what goes on. You'h not even built like Enzo. You'h too tall and too broad."

"Give me that," said Doc, snatching the hood off Raider. He put it on. "*I* could pass for him, easily."

"You're the right build," said O'Connor. "You speak the language?"

"Of course. *Si* and . . ." He shook his head.

Raider snatched the hood back. "It's my idea, I go to the meeting."

"This is insane," said Montaigne. "It's much too risky. Nobody should go."

"It's wild, sure," said Doc. "I could walk in and—"

"Come out feet first," interrupted Raider.

Doc gave him a jaundiced look. "But if you went in you'd come out with the whole pack in one rope, right? Frank, Captain, we can't let this opportunity go by. Dave's murder, losing that envelope wrecks everything. This may be a chance to salvage something. Think about it. As Rade says, they'll be expecting Enzo with the good news that Hennessey's out of the way, off their backs for good. That alone involves the whole crew in complicity to murder. It'll be the latest news, it's got to be on the agenda. They'll be discussing other business."

"Like who's gonna get it next," said Raider dourly. "You and me."

Doc tilted his head, his expression acknowledging this possibility.

"And George Provenzano has to be close to the top of the list," he said. "If we can't get his envelope back, we're going to have to tell him what's happened. They're going to turn the state upside down looking for him."

"They already are," ventured Montaigne.

Doc didn't hear him. He was too busy warming to his idea. "I'd hear every word. I could collect a ton of information for Luzenberg. I could testify. With or without Provenzano's records, his testimony together with what I'd find out, between us we'd massacre them in court."

"You first have to get there alive," said O'Connor. "I don't know, friend, you'd be taking an awful chance."

"Committing suicide," growled Raider. "Forget it. You're not going. It's my idea, I'll go. You can wait outside with fifty guns. I'll be packing mine under my cloak. If the balloon goes up, I'll fire two shots. That'll be the signal. You boys come pouring in shooting up a storm."

"No, no, no, no, no!" Doc shook his head.

Everybody was suddenly talking at once. Montaigne finally got the conversation under control. He offered a litany of suggestions. He would see to supplying the men, enlisting the help of other precincts. He reminded them of the vital importance of recovering the manila envelope. It was also his view that Doc, not Raider, be the one to attempt to infiltrate the meeting. Fortunately or unfortunately.

"Depending on youah point of view, he's almost perfect physically to stand in for Enzo. Raidah, you'ah built about as much like him as youah friend, Emma Pickett. You'd make two of him."

"Horseshit! Whose idea is it? Answer me that. Whose?"

"Patience," said O'Connor, grinning. "We'll save the next suicide mission for you."

"You're funny as a busted crotch, you know that?"

"Take it easy, Rade," said Doc consolingly. "When this whole song and dance is wrapped up and we put in for medals, we'll see you get a nice big, shiny one. Right, Frank?"

Raider snorted. "You tell 'em, wiseass! Just don't forget

one thing: You go in there and get your gullet slit or your head blown off, don't come running to me!"

He started for the door.

"Where are you going?"

"To try that bastard one more time. I might be able to scare something outta him that could save your goddamn neck. What to do while you're in there, what not—"

"Don't break anything," cautioned Montaigne. "I'd prefer to delivah him to the D.A. in one piece."

Raider dismissed the three of them with both hands and went out.

CHAPTER ELEVEN

Doc was scared. He had known real, abiding fear before not a few times, but a speedy assessment of all past dangerous situations in which he had been involved, with and without Raider, fell into the long shadow of the present one confronting him. His hood would be his only protection. The gun shoved into his belt would only delay his execution, only take a couple of them with him when the rest sent him on the long journey into darkness. The biggest, most nagging question in his mind was, once inside, would he be able to keep his hood on until he was back outside? Or, when the meeting was over, as a matter of procedure, did everyone present remove their hood? Most likely. In such an eventuality, Raider suggested he duck out.

"To go to the bathroom. Then climb out the window."

He had made it sound so easy, but at the moment, standing across the street in the shadows, watching the members of the Supreme Council arrive in twos and threes and by themselves, everyone in street clothes, carrying bundles under their arms, the task confronting him appeared anything but easy. The immediate problem, first and foremost, was how to get through the front door without the concealment of his hood. A thought came to mind. Not an extraordinary idea, not one accompanied by any guarantee of safety, but worth a try. Possibly because it was the only idea he could come up with.

As he studied the house, Raider, O'Connor, Montaigne, eight detectives, and forty uniformed officers were assembling in the backyard of a house a block away, preparatory to surrounding Esposito's house. Unfortunately, Raider had been unable to elicit anything from Enzo that might prove helpful. Doc had left the station, running all the way to Chartres Street, and easily located the house, thanks to Billy Cobb's description, which had previously been related to Raider. He had arrived with sixteen minutes to spare. Three minutes after he'd gotten there and taken up his present station the first Council members showed up, getting out of a hansom and approaching the front door. He watched as they were admitted.

Up to four minutes before ten he counted eighteen arrivals. One more, then he would step out of the shadows, cross the street, approach the door, and go in.

"My God, what am I doing? Talk about walking into the lion's mouth..."

One more minute added itself to the mountain of time pushed by the present into the past. A second one followed, the tiny hand in the shirt-button-sized circle at the bottom of the face of his Waterbury watch completing its circle. The nineteenth member of the Supreme Council appeared, coming jauntily up the walk. He turned, approached the door, knocked, went inside.

Doc followed. Confronted by the door, fist upraised to knock, he noticed the knocker and pounded it twice. The door started to open. He slipped on his hood, his cloak still draped over one arm. A tall, frigid-eyed black man nodded and stood aside. The house was an ordinary colonial, the living room to the left, the long wall interrupted by a marble fireplace, the dining room to the right, a stairway ascending to the second floor directly in front of him. He could hear voices below. Ignoring the servant, he started down them, donning his cloak, tying the silken cord across the front just under his chin as he descended.

Reaching the bottom, he waited a long moment outside, off to one side of the opened door. Then, taking a deep breath, he swept in. His heart jumped in his chest, twisting slightly, he imagined, before settling back into place. To his immense relief, the dice tossed had come up winning: Everyone present had on their hoods and dominoes.

The room resembled a medieval torture chamber without the devices. Illumination was provided by a dozen three-foot candles. The walls were bare, wet stone, the floor, dirt, the ceiling rafters hung with spider webs and heavily shadowed. Four long tables were set up end to end along one wall, with chairs behind them; he counted seventeen. Opposite stood a podium, and behind it an altar. Before the podium was a small table; on it, a human skull with twin daggers inserted in the eye sockets. On either side of the skull stood candles. Above the altar, on the rear wall, hung a large scroll inscribed in Italian. Even with his fair knowledge of Latin, he could not make out a word of it, except to note that the first letters of the last five words were capitalized: M, A, F, I, A.

The Council members stood about in small groups, talking in low tones. He drifted into the room.

"Buona sera," said a man behind him.

He turned. *"Buona sera."*

The eyes in the hood held him. He could sense that the man was preparing to start up a conversation. In Italian, he thought, his heart sinking. Then a door opened alongside the altar and three men came out, two in black hoods and dominoes, the third entirely in white. The latter, the shortest of the three, took his place at the podium, the other two standing behind chairs flanking him.

Under the arm of the man at the podium was Hennessey's manila envelope. He raised his gavel, then pounded it twice. The members took their seats, Doc taking pains to be the last to sit. The two who had come in with Esposito—Doc assumed that the man with the gavel was he—took their seats on either side of him. He laid the envelope unopened on the podium and proceeded to call attendance.

"Bastion Incardona!"

"Qui."

"Carlo Matranga!"

"Qui."

"Antonio Matranga!"

"Qui."

And so on. Once more Doc's heart sank. Evidently, the entire meeting was to be conducted in Italian. So much for all the "dynamite information" he had earlier bragged he would get. Two things only appeared obtainable. By some miracle as yet unrevealed to him, he must get his hands on the envelope. Secondly, almost equally miraculous, he must get himself out alive.

"Antonio Scafedi!"

"Qui."

"Joseph Madreca!"

"Qui."

"Joseph Provenzano!"

Doc started, almost jumping up from his seat. Good God!

"Qui."

George's brother, a member of the Supreme Council? Could there be *two* Joseph Provenzanos? Impossible. Like a flight of arrows, questions impinged on his mind. Did George know? Good God, was he also a member? No, he had to be on the up and up. Why else would the envelope have to be stolen? Would those present hold Joe accountable for George's actions? Was he even aware of what his brother was up to? He was now or would be shortly, reflected Doc, eyeing the envelope lying on the podium. Complications were suddenly rolling in and tangling, forming a huge knot.

"Enzo Carlone!"

Doc reacted.

"En—"

"Qui."

"Pietro Monasterio!"

"Qui."

Esposito began to speak, holding up the envelope and summoning Joe Provenzano to stand before the skull impaled with the two daggers. Esposito read excerpts from the contents of the envelope. His listeners reacted in astonishment. One spoke up. He was silenced and mildly reprimanded. Esposito addressed Joe directly. Doc could not make out, not even guess at what either was saying, but it was obviously a discussion of the problem at hand. They finished talking and Joe resumed his place. Esposito went on to other matters.

"Enzo Carlone!"

Doc swallowed hard, got to his feet, slipped behind Pietro Monasterio's chair, and took Joe's place before the podium. The skull grinned up at him. He imagined the jaw hinges loosening, the mouth moving, speaking:

"Imbecile! Here you are, trapped! Two doors, the one you came in, the one he came in. Both locked. You're dead, Weatherbee. What are you standing there for, you think you can buy time? Don't be foolish. Why prolong the agony? How long do you think you can fool them? One question in Italian, you won't understand a syllable. One little question. How do you answer? How will you fake it? Down he'll come from his podium, whip off your hood, and you can start counting the seconds till you're dead! You won't get to six.

"Why go through all that? Be smart, take your hood off, show your face, get it over with."

Agony it was. Doc could feel sweat running down his face, burning his eyes, setting them itching. He felt clamminess in the palms of his hands. His armpits were soaked. The sweat running down inside his arms tickled. He stiffened his legs to keep his knees from trembling, knocking.

Esposito was carrying on loudly. From his tone of voice, he appeared to be praising him. The members behind him voiced agreement, approval. He was the hero of the moment. Why shouldn't he be? Hadn't he helped remove the biggest single obstacle to the organization's continued domination of the city?

Suddenly, the man in white stopped. Coming down from his podium, he stood to one side and placed his hands on Doc's shoulders. He kissed him through the hood on both cheeks. The onlookers broke into applause. Esposito patted him on the back, the signal that he should return to his seat. He took it as a signal and did so. Another man and still another were summoned to receive official congratulations on a job well done. Enzo's two companions, reflected Doc ruefully.

The meeting continued for another half hour, members standing up in turn, getting instructions from Esposito, yielding the place of honor to the next man.

"Enzo Carlone!"

Doc almost said *"qui,"* catching himself just in time. He got to his feet, his heart pumping even more violently than before. He stiffened to keep from trembling. Esposito addressed him. At the end of each sentence Doc nodded. Three words only he could understand. Nevertheless, the man in white's instructions were abundantly clear. Thanks to his success in dealing with David Hennessey, he, Enzo Carlone, was to be accorded the honor, assigned the job of assassinating Operatives Raider and Weatherbee.

The three words that clarified his orders to him: *duo*. Pingar-tuns. *Assassino*.

Esposito rattled the podium with his gavel. Everyone rose and together repeated an oath. Doc mumbled along, setting his index finger against his temple, raising his hand palm out to shoulder height, covering his heart with his hand, always a split-second behind the others, but this went unnoticed.

The oath completed, the meeting was adjourned. Doc froze. Everyone was on his feet, mingling, removing their hoods. He reached for the top of his own, at the same time easing slowly toward the door through which he had entered. He cast a last covetous look at the envelope lying on the podium. There wasn't a chance in hell of getting hold of it, he decided. To do so he would have to cover the thirty feet to the podium, grab it, and return to the door. Moving forth and back through practically the entire assembly. Not to mention running up the stairs, getting out of the house, and, once outside, out of pistol range on legs filled to his knees with water.

He made it to the door and started up the stairs, walking leisurely, advertising none of his panic. Two men stuck their heads out below him. He recognized Joe Provenzano.

"Congratulazione, Enzo!" called Joe, beaming.

"Grazi, grazi," he murmured.

Both men frowned, asking with their eyes why he was still wearing his hood, he told himself. But neither said anything. They waved, turned, and reentered the room.

He walked out of the house and crossed the street. He began walking faster down it and broke into a run, running, running. He heard steps behind him. He ran faster.

"Doc! Doc!"

It was Raider with O'Connor and Montaigne. Doc stopped

short and collapsed, his knees buckling. Raider came running up.

"What's the matter? You okay? What happened back there? What the hell's the matter with you? You hit?"

"Just shut up and let me sit here. Let me catch my breath."

Raider turned to the others: uniforms massed in a semicircle behind them, men brandishing their nightsticks and staring curiously.

"They're leaving that place," burst out Raider. "Let's get back and round 'em up. Doc, they're leaving, right?"

"Don't go back, don't do anything."

"What have we got to hold them on?" asked Montaigne.

Raider paid no attention. He knelt beside his partner. "Did you get back the envelope?"

"No."

"Why not? What happened?"

"Will you stop asking questions! Will you stop breathing on me! Frank, can you go back with a half-dozen men and search the house?"

"I got a search warrant, just in case." He waved the document.

"What about the bigwigs?" pressed Raider.

Doc glared impatiently. "We already told you, there's nothing to hold them on. Suspicions just aren't enough. Their lawyers'd spring them in an hour. Frank, that envelope's got to be in there somewhere. Turn the place upside down if you have to."

"Right."

He left with O'Connor and ten others. Raider got to his feet, preparing to follow.

"You stay here, Rade." Doc got up with his partner's help.

"You okay, Doc?"

"Lovely, considering I've just spent an hour of my life looking down into the pit."

"What happened?"

Doc filled in between his entering and his leaving.

"Provenzano's brother's one of 'em?" Raider shook his head in disbelief. "Brother against brother . . ."

"There's more. Guess what? I got instructions to murder you and me."

"Oh, bullshit!"

Doc raised his hand. "Cross my heart, hope to die. What am I saying!" Dusting off his trousers, he glanced about. Not a soul could be seen, apart from the majority of uniforms still remaining, standing about awaiting further orders. "Let's get out of here. I need a drink. I need a bottle!"

Montaigne, O'Connor, and the others went over every inch of Esposito's house, but there was no sign of the envelope. In questioning Mr. Hair, every time Montaigne mentioned the envelope, Esposito would laugh, leading the lieutenant and O'Connor to suspect that he had put a match to it.

Losing Exhibit A was a heavy blow to the state's case; losing George Provenzano promised even heavier. Raider and Doc decided to catch the midnight train up to Slidell, change there for Mandeville, arrive, and walk back to Hennessey's cabin.

Montaigne gave them directions and wished them luck. Doc felt a professional obligation to include him in their plans.

"George is probably safe there with Donahue and Forzaglia," he said. The four of them were standing outside Montaigne's office. "Still, I think we ought to look over the area. We might find a better place."

"The mob's been combing the state looking for him evah since they got theah. I don't see how moving him to another place is going to do anything good foh us. Or him."

"Maybe not," said Raider looking at his partner questioningly.

"We'll decide on it when we get there," said Doc.

"Are you going to tell him what happened to his envelope?" O'Connor asked.

Doc nodded. "I think we have to. He's been straight with us. We owe him the same treatment, don't we?"

"You tell him and he'll toss in the sponge," said Montaigne. "That'll be the crushah. With the envelope gone, he's all we've got left."

"We got the small fry," ventured Raider. "We got Enzo. We got what you found out, Doc."

"That and a nickel'll buy you a cigar, Rade. All I got was Joe Provenzano."

"I hate to say it," said O'Connor, "but your case looks to be in fairly rotten shape. You might start thinking about a postponement."

"That's up to Luzenberg and Mayah Shakespeah," said Montaigne. He opened his office door and glanced at his clock. "If you two are going, you'd bettah go. You've got nine minutes to catch the Slidell train."

CHAPTER TWELVE

No sooner were they settled in their seat then it began drizzling outside. The drops formed darts, slashing the window in a diagonal pattern as the train pulled out of the station, picking up speed. There were only seven other passengers in the car. They had purposely selected a seat as far from the other occupants as they could get, so that they could talk without putting their heads together, keeping their voices down, and giving the general impression of two men conspiring to hold up the train.

Raider groaned, stretched, and settled back, kicking his boots off. "I sure hope old George is okay."

"He's fine. This case should be in as good shape. Say, something just occurred to me. Do you know, I haven't the faintest idea what my time limit is?"

"What are you talking 'bout?"

"How long I have to assassinate us. Esposito must have set a time limit, only in Italian."

"You're funny." Raider shook his head. "What I can't get over is the Provenzanos. One brother helping us out, practically

107

holding up the damn case single-handed, like the statue o' the guy with the world on his shoulders."

"Atlas, Rade."

"Whatever, and the other, a kingpin on the other side. You think George suspects?"

"Who knows? Isn't it amazing how much has happened in the short time since he, Forzaglia, and Donahue left?"

Mention of the two policemen put a sour expression on Raider's face. It became one of disbelief. "Brother against brother."

"That intrigues you, doesn't it?"

"I never had a brother. Guys who don't likely think more 'bout the bond between brothers, what it is, what it should be, what it stands for than them that have brothers."

"That's a fairly profound observation, Rade. It might even be true. They're going to be facing each other in court. That should be interesting."

"Providin' this thing ever gets to court."

It was raining harder, the window rendered opaque by the dart pattern. The car smelled of coal dust. It was dim and dingy and shook and rattled passing over every rail gap.

They reached Slidell within seconds of one o'clock by Doc's watch, chugging and clanking into the little, darkened station. The Abita Springs train, to which they would be changing and which would drop them at Mandeville, was waiting, a locomotive and four cars. They boarded in the rain with other passengers. The train pulled out hooting mournfully. They passed through tiny Bayou Lacombe and presently reached Mandeville. They were the only two passengers to get off. It had stopped raining, but the sky continued overcast. Everything was damp and shining, the ground muddy, the air heavy with moisture. Lake Pontchartrain wasn't actually a lake at all, but a landlocked saltwater bay, its waters rising and falling with the tides. It was surrounded by grasslands. They started down the road, back the way their train had come, following Frank Montaigne's directions to Hennessey's cottage. Doc carried Enzo's satchel, in which was packed a large-size policeman's uniform and other items. Raider, walking ahead of him, turned and eyed the satchel with evident disapproval.

"That bag's a fairly dumb idea, if you ask me."

"I wasn't aware I had, Rade. It doesn't concern you. It's for George to accept or reject it."

"Montaigne's right. You tell him what's happened, he'll toss in the sponge. See if he doesn't. Want to bet cash money?"

"No, and see that you let me do the talking. You promised."

"Oh, hell yes. It's your show, I won't say a word."

"Try not to show him your face. I know you, you'll sit there with pessimism, discouragement written all over it."

"How 'bout I wear my hat over it. Would that suit Your Majesty?"

Doc didn't answer. They walked along, listening to the voices of the night, the stridulation of marsh creatures, frogs voicing their presence, the occasional shrill cry of a hawk wandered from its home in the forest or a cypress swamp. Doc hurried his step, coming alongside Raider.

"Any wild animals here, you think?"

"Sure, man-eating snapping clams, snapping turtles with jaws like a mountain cat. How much further you figure?"

"A half mile is a half mile."

"Hold it right there!" barked a voice out of the darkness to their right. "Get 'em up high."

They obliged, Doc dropping the satchel. A uniformed policeman emerged from the tall grass, waving a shotgun. Dennis Donahue. He recognized Raider.

"You!"

"Lower that thing, damn it! It could go off!" Donahue complied. Raider introduced Doc, then glanced about them questioningly. "Where in hell is this place?"

"Follow me."

He led the way into the grass, down a pathway they could only feel, not see, the grass rising almost to their hips. He regaled them with a long recital of how efficiently, how conscientiously he and his partner had been guarding Provenzano, spelling each other off around the clock. Presently, they could hear the light splashing of fish leaping for flies. A small house rose up before them against the sky, slender rods of light trimming the edges of the fully drawn shades of two front windows.

"How is George doing?" Doc asked.

"Great. He and Forzaglia play checkers for hours at a time. Zag and me take turns going into Mandeville to pick up a New

Orleans paper every day. Provenzano's been fishing, too. He likes the canoe. He likes it out here. It's okay, except it gets damp as hell nights."

"Anybody come nosing round?" asked Raider.

"Not a soul. It's been quiet as the grave."

Raider grunted. Doc grinned to himself.

"What's going on back in the city?" Donahue asked.

"Hennessey got himself murdered," said Raider blandly, in a tone that suggested the chief had stubbed his toe.

Donahue's gasp came back at them out of the darkness. Doc, bringing up the rear, tapped Raider's shoulder, shaking his head at him, signaling his request to let him explain, hoping to inject a little sensitivity into the subject. He briefly detailed what had happened in Basin Street. They came up to the house. Donahue knocked.

"Who is it?" asked a voice inside.

"Governor Sam." Donahue turned to them, his expression proud like that of a small boy who had just won at marbles, mused Doc. "That's the password."

Raider rolled his eyes but said nothing. The door opened slowly. Forzaglia had his jacket off, his service revolver in hand, his eyes troubled, curious at sight of the Pinkertons. George was sitting at a checkerboard, the game half completed. He was in his long johns, his feet bare. A basin half filled with soapy water was on the floor alongside the overturned wooden bucket serving as a table for the checkerboard. He had been washing his feet; they were pink and shining.

The cottage was sparely furnished, necessities only, the windows curtainless, the floor bare boards. It was suprisingly neat, reflected Doc. Overhead, shelves were lined with canned food. Fishing gear was hung on a line of coat hooks. There was a pump at the sink. There was also a wooden bench, a small table, and chairs. Identical doors, both closed, led to back rooms. Bedrooms, he thought, probably double-decker bunks with straw ticks.

"They got Hennessey," rasped Donahue. "Gunned him down in cold blood!"

George shot to his feet, upsetting the board, scattering the checkers. His eyes welled with fear. "'S not true!" he gasped.

"It is, it is!" insisted Donahue. "It's what happened, didn't it, fellows? Tell him..."

Doc cut him off with a wave. "Take it easy, George," he said soothingly. "It's true. He's been killed, ambushed. They tried and tried to get him and finally . . . But," he added hastily, "you're in no danger. You're going to be more protected than ever. We're closing in on them. The case is going before the grand jury in just a few days."

George had been backing off slowly. Reaching behind him, he took his trousers down from a hook. He started getting into them. "Jesus, this is awful, terrible!"

"Has anybody come nosin' round here?" Raider asked him.

"No, but—"

"Then this place is safe, right? You're safe."

"Here maybe, not back in town. Not in no courtroom. Hennessey . . . I can't believe it!"

Doc calmed him down. Forzaglia appeared as stunned by the news as George. Only Donahue was blasé about it. He stirred the fire, adding wood to the squat little stove to heat coffee.

They sat sipping in silence, watching Forzaglia put his jacket on and go out to stand guard. Doc eyed George over the lip of his tin cup. The big man appeared to have calmed down considerably. He sat combing his beard with his fingers, his head down, his eyes on the floor between his bare feet.

"George, Chief Hennessey had your evidence on him when he was shot."

"They got it," said Raider.

"We searched Esposito's house, but there was no sign of it," said Doc. "We think he destroyed it."

Raising his shaggy head, George looked from one to the other. From his eyes he seemed to Doc to be weighing the seriousness of the loss. He finally shrugged, his expression becoming almost jaunty.

"That's no big problem." He tapped the side of his head. "I got it all up here, just about. All that's important. I wrote it all once, I can write it again."

"You think you can remember everything, the whole envelope?" asked Raider incredulously. "All those dates?"

"Sure." He shifted his eyes to Doc. "Who shot Hennessey?"

"We think there were three of them. We only got one, Enzo Carlone."

"Easy."

"I beg your pardon?"

"That's what they call him. He's a phony bastard. Hangs around Tony Matranga's saloon. He's a finger man. Never pulls the trigger, just goes along to spot who's gonna get it."

Doc studied the bottom of his cup, retasting the coffee, the flavor lingering, slightly bitter in his mouth.

"George, there's something else you should know. I got into a meeting of the Supreme Council. When Enzo was arrested he was carrying this satchel here with his hood and cloak. I put them on and took his place."

"Mister, you got balls!"

"George, your brother was at the meeting."

George laughed, ridiculing such a suggestion. *"Your* brother, maybe, not mine. Cut the bullshit."

"Your brother, George. Do you know any other Joe Provenzanos?"

"There ain't any, not in New Orleans." His face hardened. "Hey, what is this, you trying to be funny?"

"He's not," said Raider. "He's telling you what he saw, what he knows firsthand. Joe's in with them. He's one o' the big boys."

George heard this and said nothing further in the way of denial. His grin dissolved into a frown of disbelief that deepened, darkening. Slowly he lowered his eyes, then his head. The wheels were turning, Doc noted, spinning faster and faster, weighing the disclosure. He appeared to be struggling, his brain, his intelligence wrestling his heart, brimming, overflowing with filial love. He shook his head with the finality of a judge denying a stay of execution.

"You lie in your damn teeth!"

"It's the truth," said Doc. "I was there, I saw him, I heard his name in the roll call. I heard him speak. Even with a hood on, I couldn't mistake his voice. Why would I lie about such a thing? What could I gain? You're already on our side. Do you think I came all the way up here to bait you? All I want is for everything to be out in the open, good and bad."

George heard, but made no response, not even shaking his head or nodding. No movement whatsoever. He continued to avert his eyes, avoiding Doc's. Then he took a breath, his massive shoulders shuddering slightly. The turmoil within was building; any second now it would explode. He would shoot

to his feet and begin ranting, storming about. Doc tensed.
Donahue and Raider were staring at George. Slowly he got up,
turning his back on them, speaking so softly Doc could scarcely
make out what he was saying.

"Joe. Big brother. Brother, friend, pal. My idol my whole
life." He turned. Tears glistened, setting his cheeks shining,
rolling down into his beard. "My idol, that's what he was when
we were kids growing up together. When I got in trouble it
was always Joe got me out. When a big guy come after me it
was Joe who'd take him on, save my hide. He got into more
fights over me and Peter than over anything *he* ever did. He
protected us like a big brother should, you know? He was
always there, always ready. He made us feel safe, *capish?*

"He made us so proud of him. We looked up to him so.
Our hero, you know? He was like having a whole army on
your side, protecting you, guarding you. Joe. You love a woman;
I love my Maria. I love my kids. But the love you have for
your brother, that's different. It's, you know, special. It lasts
your whole life.

"I believe Joe's in with them. The pieces fit, *capish?* I think
back, whenever we talked about what they were doing to us,
how we had to pay and pay, the times they'd strong-arm us.
I'd get so mad. I'd yell and threaten. All noise. Never did
nothing; nothing you could do. But thinking back, *he* never
got mad, never got that look in *his* eye, you know, like fire,
hate, boiling mad. He'd just shrug it off. And look, you know,
sheepish. He'd never look me in the eye. I'd say I'm gonna
get a gun and go after Charlie and Tony, shoot the bastards, I
don't care if they hang me for it. I said it so many times, I
can't remember how many. But never once did he say 'I'm
with you,' or even 'That's no good' and, you know, warn me
against going off crazy. He never said nothing. All he ever did
was put his arm around my shoulders and say 'Take it easy,
take it easy.' Everything was 'take it easy,' every problem,
every headache, squeeze. 'Take it easy, George, it's only
money.'

"You ask yourself, you know? How can a guy who's so
tough, a guy you grew up in the same house with and you
know like you know yourself, who knocks the block off every
bully in the neighborhood... Hey, he was twelve, thirteen
years old, he goes after a grown man who tries to give Pop a

hard time, you know? How can a guy that tough be so weak when they put the screws to us? He's no yellow-belly. How come? How can he just fork over and turn his back on it. How can he say 'Take it easy, it's only money'? He must have said that a hundred times. Sure he could pay up and take it easy. So could you if you knew you were getting it back." He rubbed his fingers against his palm.

"When the net is pulled in..." began Doc.

"Joe'll be in it with the rest. I know, I know. So? What am I supposed to do, back down? I mean, who's wrong, him or me? Not me. I'm no saint, but I'm not one o' them. Neither was Peter. He was so clean... Mama used to call him St. Peter, *capish?*"

He paused, searching their eyes. "They'll lock Joe up for the rest of his life, won't they?"

"Probably," said Doc.

"He could hang," said Donahue.

Doc glared at him fiercely.

"Why don't you clam up!" exclaimed Raider heatedly. "Nobody's asking you."

"Sorry," mumbled Donahue.

"He's right." George nodded. "I'll be putting a rope around my own brother's neck."

"Not you, George, not even the state. Whatever happens to him he'll have only himself to thank for it," said Doc. "And it's going to happen. They're doomed. The mob is finished in New Orleans."

George chuckled mirthlessly. "I know. So Hennessey was always saying."

CHAPTER THIRTEEN

George Provenzano's reaction to his visitors' bad news, his attitude, his continuing loyalty to the cause, came as a relief to Raider and Doc. It was clear to everyone, however, that having secured and probably destroyed the contents of the envelope, the mob would now go all out to locate George and silence him. Brother Joe would know how damaging his testimony could be. It was true that George couldn't do any damage until the case came before the grand jury, but neither Pinkerton saw this as any reason to assume that he would be completely safe away from New Orleans. As George himself said, the man who killed him would be as big a hero as the ones who had ambushed Hennessey.

Doc had come to Lake Pontchartrain with an unusual bit of strategy in mind for protecting their star witness. His idea was to "make the protected one of the protectors." He asked George to shave off his beard and mustache and put on the policeman's uniform he had brought along. He selected his partner to play

George, including in the contents of the satchel a false beard and mustache. George was physically bigger than Raider—two inches taller, and broader through the chest and shoulders—but Doc pointed out that in George's clothes, wearing a beard, mustache, and sideburns, Raider could pass for the fruit importer at a distance. Hopefully, anyone coming after George would not get close enough to perceive that he had a stand-in.

George liked the idea. Raider, for the obvious reason, was less than enthusiastic.

"If I told you once, I've told you fifteen hundred times, I purely can't stand phony face hair. It itches me like hell!" he fumed.

"You afraid you're going to get your head blown off?" asked George.

"No, no, no, that's not it at all."

George laughed in his face and walked off into his bedroom.

"Rade, can't you cooperate just this once?" Casting a worried eye at the partially opened bedroom door, Doc lowered his voice. "Somebody's going to be showing up here, you know that."

"That's why he's playing so hard to get," called George from the bedroom. Laughter followed. Raider sneered and made a fist at the door.

"All right, all right, all right," he grumbled. "Give me the goddamn hair!"

"It's just for a few days. I went to the meeting, didn't I? This is the least you can do."

"Will you stop talking 'bout that goddamn meeting? So you're a hero. Congratulations. What do you want me to do, put up a damn statue in Jackson Square? Tell me something, what are you gonna be doing while I'm playing target?"

"I, ah..."

Raider cupped his ear. "I can't hear you, Did you say something?"

"I have to go back, obviously."

"You mean you're just gonna leave me here?"

"Oh, stop it. You make it sound like I'm deserting you."

"What do you call it, for chrissakes!"

"I've *got* to go back, you know that." He lowered his voice even further. "Frank Montaigne is about as eager to go to court as Esposito."

"He could be right, with what's been happening and all."

"He's dead wrong. And the D.A.'s not that eager. The mayor is, thank the Lord. I'm going back there and get together with him and push for a trial for all I'm worth."

"I bet you a quarter Montaigne'll try to talk you into waiting."

"What's the point in waiting? What's really changed? Rade, the longer we wait . . ." He paused, nodding toward George's bedroom door.

"The riskier it is for him," said Raider. "I know. Only starting now it's not him, *I'm* him. I'm the one gets it when the damn shooting starts."

"Okay." Doc snatched the cluster of false facial hair from him. "You go back and talk to Shakespeare, I'll play George."

Raider snatched back. "You're too damn small. Your coloring's all wrong. I'm doing it. Chrissakes, if I don't, nobody else will, that's for sure." An idea brightened his face. "Hey, how 'bout Donahue? He's big enough."

"We need his gun outside, stupid. And his partner's."

George appeared in the doorway, every inch the uniformed policeman. "Mine, too. I can handle a gun. How's this for a perfect fit?"

"You look great," said Doc. "All you have to do now is shave."

"Everything? Even my mustache?"

"Mustache, beard, sideburns, the works. When's the last time you were clean-shaven?"

"When I was a kid. Seventeen, eighteen. Years ago, half a lifetime."

"Good. Even your best friend won't recognize you."

"Joe will, in a minute."

Raider snorted. "They're not gonna send your own brother after you."

"Oh no? You don't know Esposito. He's got what you call—"

"A sense of irony?" inquired Doc.

"He loves to play with people, you know, like they're little pieces on a game board. Checkers. Only there's only one king."

• • •

Doc had entered the imposing Ionic temple of City Hall surrounding Lafayette Square, had followed the signs to the mayor's office, but once arrived was informed that he would be obliged to wait until the meeting of the Sewage and Water Board was over. He sat outside for an hour before those in attendance came filing out of the office. Mayor Shakespeare appeared, grinning, extending his hand.

"I apologize. We're in the midst of a big drainage job and out of money as usual. We're trying to rob Peter to pay Paul. But you didn't come to hear my troubles." He sobered. "I was shocked and appalled when I heard what happened. David was one of the finest public servants this city has ever had. I've never met anyone I respected more. I appointed him to the job, you know. He'll be missed. Now then, come in, come in, we'll get you a nice, comfortable chair, all warmed up, a little something to take the edge off the day." He winked. "Miss Elberon, no interruptions, please," he said to his aging, dyed-blond secretary.

The office was enormous, a barn of a place, the four ceiling lamps descending from at least forty feet above. Tall windows looked out upon Lafayette Square. His Honor's desk looked to be half the size of a railroad flatcar and was piled with file folders, books, and correspondence. He moved to a sideboard.

"What'll it be? Bourbon, scotch? I have some excellent sherry. Manzanilla, dry as a bone. How about a glass?"

"Thank you, Mr. Mayor."

So dry was the sherry, for a fleeting moment Doc feared that his tongue would cleave to the roof of his mouth. Dry, but delicious, excellent. They lit cigars. The mayor settled back in his posture chair.

"Where do we stand now, with David out of the picture? Incidentally, I've put Lieutenant Montaigne in temporary charge of the investigation. He doesn't have the rank, of course. He was a sergeant only last week. But he was David's right hand. He knows this case backwards and forwards."

"Good choice, good man."

"Let's hope." Shakespeare studied him. "He seems a trifle reluctant to put this mess before the grand jury. I disagree. David's death doesn't change anything. I've already asked Charlie Luzenberg to draw up his indictments. I want to get this through the grand jury to formal arraignment as fast as we can, don't you agree?"

"Definitely. We're sitting on George Provenzano. He's willing to testify, he's ready. The longer we wait, the harder it'll be on him. On all of us."

"David's funeral is to be held from the Council Chamber here in City Hall. Prominent citizens from all over the state will be paying their respects. Public indignation is as high as I've ever seen it in all my years in this town. There's a lot of talk of lynching going around. So much that a number of our decent, law-abiding Italian citizens have taken to publishing notices in the newspapers disavowing any connection with the Mafia or the suspects the police have rounded up. As of last count, we have twenty-one suspects under lock and key. You've probably heard that I've appointed a Citizens Committee of Fifty, prominent New Orleanians who'll be helping the police to gather evidence."

"Do you think they'll come up with anything?"

Shakespeare scoffed. "Of course not! They'll raise a lot of hot air, fill the newspapers with their pronouncements, and eventually fade into the woodwork. But the avowed purpose of any such committee is almost never its real purpose. The idea is to keep public indignation high.

"By the way, did you know that the police found the gun that killed David? Double-barreled shotgun, cut down the way the Dagos do. Found in the gutter near a shed across the street from David's house. The shots appear to have been fired from the shed. They're still looking for the shell casings. You know, I can't for the life of me understand Montaigne and Charlie Luzenberg, and others I could name. You'd think they'd be breaking down the doors to get this thing into court."

"It's going to be complicated. They want to win. Your friend the D.A. would prefer to leave very little to chance. Listening to him at lunch that day at your house, I got the feeling that it's not so much that he's afraid to go into court with what we have, it's that he's waiting for something."

"For what, the big panjandrum's signed confession? It's time he understood we've got to take the bull by the horns."

"I agree, so does my partner."

"Where is Raider, by the way?"

Doc explained.

"Well, like you say, we sure can't keep Provenzano sitting up at the lake till doomsday. I'll get in touch with Charlie. The funeral's tomorrow. The day after we're going to the grand jury. I mean it!"

Down came his fist, jiggling his sherry. Doc smiled inwardly. It was precisely what he'd come all the way back to hear.

CHAPTER FOURTEEN

George and Raider seemed to gravitate toward each other, and with so much time on their hands and so little to do, particularly after nightfall, they fell into long conversations over the checkerboard, the Pinkerton taking over for Forzaglia, who admitted having become bored with the game.

Raider had never placed a very high value on tact. In his code of human relationships it came too close to deceit to be useful. Whenever a question that interested him popped into his head he didn't hesitate to ask it, even if it might embarrass the answerer. Where Doc would have thought twice, Raider considered once was enough. Spontaneous outburst was honesty in action.

Doc had returned to the city, Donahue was in his bunk snoring, and Forzaglia was outside on guard the night following the Pinkertons' arrival. Raider and George were bent over the checkerboard, the game just about to be decided, when a question popped into the loser's head.

"Tell me, George, you and Joe and Peter were partners, you

and Joe still. Joe handles the books, right? The bucks?"

"Leo Rastelli is the bookkeeper."

"Did Joe hire him?"

"A long time ago, when we first started."

"Is this Rastelli one of the Matrangas' people?"

"He wasn't, back when he started with us. I can't say now."
He finished setting up his checkers for the next game and then
paused, looking up at his opponent. "I don't even know where
my own brother stands, how can I know about anybody else?
That's what makes it all so rotten, you know? You can't trust
anybody. Everybody wears two goddamn faces."

"You don't. There's gotta be a lot working for you don't."

"Yeah." His tone carried little conviction. "A lot, maybe
two or three, too small or too green for the mob to bother
about."

"If Rastelli keeps your books, he'd be the one making the
payoffs, right? And finagling the figures to make it look like
everything's on the up and up."

"The payoffs are in cash. They don't show up in the books.
You ask me whether he's still our man or gone over to the
other side. He's not 'our' man, he's his, Joe's. Does that answer
your question?"

"You say Joe handles the financial end of it."

"All of it. Leo works with him. The shipping costs, sales,
all the figures. Contracts with the shippers, the percentages,
licenses . . ."

"You don't get involved in any o' that."

"That's all what we call inside work. I'm strictly outside.
I handle the labor, check the loads, schedules, arrivals, departures. But mostly the dockhands. The paymaster pays 'em.
He gets the payroll money from Leo. I take care of their time.
They punch in and out, you know? Peter used to be the time
man, but now I got to do it. Because it's outside. Anything
has to do with outside is my baby, *capish?* Peter used to spot-
check the fruit, you know? Now I do that, too. I got help, o'
course, but it's my responsibility. A ship comes in, I go aboard,
double-check the manifest, spot-check the load. Then the unloading starts. It goes on all day, all night. Out of the hold,
up on the shoulder, down the plan, across the wharf to the
boxcars.

"It's a beautiful sight, Raider, one long, green line, like a snake crawling up out of the hold, across the deck, down the gangplank, across the wharf, crawling into the boxcar. Riding shoulders all the way, Greeks, Italians, Negroes—eighty, ninety pounds up on the shoulder, light as a basket o' flowers. Beautiful. The sunlight streams down on the white ship, the green fruit, the old Negro women with white cloths tied around their heads moving up and down the line, selling sandwiches and their homemade candy, and giving water to the boys with a dipper. Smiling, happy, singing..." He swiped at his eyes with the backs of his hands. "Such a beautiful sight! Oh, and such a great business—big, profitable. Everybody eats bananas, right? New Orleans is the biggest banana port in the whole world, you know? The biggest, and Provenzano Brothers, the biggest importers." He stared misty-eyed. "Why, Raider?"

"What?"

"Why did he sell us out?"

"Pressure..."

"But did he have to become one o' them? Did he have to take on their stink and their sins? Did *they* force his hands down into the blood?"

"Who says he's got blood on his hands?"

"He's got Peter's."

"George, he didn't—"

"He's with 'em, he's one of 'em, that's all I got to know, *capish?*"

"You're forgetting one thing: He was afraid."

"Afraid? Joe? Twelve years old and he beats up a grown man for getting tough with Pop. Him, afraid? You don't know him. He's one in a million for guts. You put a knife to his throat, he'd spit on it."

"He wasn't up against one man. This is a damn snake with six hundred legs. What do you think would have happened to him if he turned 'em down?"

"I did, didn't I?"

"They didn't come to you. It was him they gave the choice to."

"But—"

"You were the lucky one. He was the one they put the collar round. And once they had him they probably figured they didn't need you. It might even have been *he* told them that. You got me, what do you need with George?

"All I'm trying to say is it's easy to say what he did was wrong. It sure wasn't right, but given the choice, he figured he couldn't beat 'em, he couldn't win. So he knuckled under."

"Knuckling under is one thing—paying off, following orders. But he didn't have to join 'em, goddamn it! He at least coulda told me before he did. He didn't. Not before, not since. Son of a bitch never said nothing!"

"Maybe he was trying to protect you."

"Bullshit." He flared at Raider. "What are you doing, making excuses for him? Protect *me?* That's *stupido!* I'm not a kid, I'm not his little brother nine years old. I don't need nobody's protection!"

"I know, I know, but it could be he still sees it like back when you both were kids. Once a big brother, always—"

"I'm none of his goddamn business, *capish? That's* how he should see it, if he wasn't such a *chooch.* I hope they hang the son of a bitch in the middle o' Lafayette Square. I'll stand in the front and cheer so loud..." He broke off, his eyes welling with tears.

"Take it easy." Raider reached across the board, placing his hand tentatively on George's arm. George shook it off.

"He killed Peter, murdered his own flesh and blood."

"Horseshit!"

"*They* killed him; he's one of 'em. He might just as well have tied the knots himself. How do you know he didn't? Tony Matranga says jump through the hoop, he jumps. *I* gotta be the biggest *chooch* in the world—deaf, dumb, and blind. I never dreamed... Practically from the day they come to us to put the heat on he's been in their pocket. They woulda run us outta town if Esposito hadn't stepped in. He told 'em to let us keep running things, only start kicking in, slice o' the pie, bigger and bigger, *capish?* And Joe was the cherry on top. The inside watchdog. He does a good job, good soldier. So good they make him a *capo,* kick him upstairs to the Supreme Council. Meantime, everything's roses on the waterfront. They milk the cow till it's practically bleeding.

"Let me tell you what I'm gonna do, Raider, when I get up on the witness stand. After I answer all the questions I'm going to ask the judge to let me tell the whole story about our family: Joe, me, and Peter, and what Joe done."

"Maybe you won't have to."

"I goddamn want to! He's gonna have to pull out a gun and shoot me to shut me up." He laughed brittlely. "We'll see how brave he is face to face. It's not gonna be like it was with Peter. He . . ."

He stopped short. A gun had gone off outside. More shots followed. They seemed to be coming from the north. Flashes of light could be seen through the kitchen windows. They ran to look out. Raider lowered one lamp to a glow the size of his thumbnail and set it on the floor. At his order, George extinguished the other, virtually darkening the interior. A wide swath of moonlight flooded the floor. More shots followed. Donahue came stumbling out of the bedroom, his jacket unbuttoned, his hair awry. He had his pistol out and open and was checking, making sure it was fully loaded.

"What the hell's going on?" he asked, bleary-eyed.

"It sounds like shooting," said Raider dryly. "You and George button up and get out there and give him some help."

Donahue stared. "What about you?"

"I'm supposed to be the one you're protecting, remember?"

"They want to take this place. They'll come bustin' in."

"Take it easy. We don't even know for certain it's them. That's why you've gotta go out. If it is, your partner's gonna need help."

"It's them, isn't it?" said Donahue evenly.

"Good bet," said Raider.

"How could it be?" George asked. "Nobody knows I'm here."

"Think about it," said Raider. "Folks know this place belongs to Hennessey. *They* now know you're playing ball with him. They know you're hiding out someplace."

More shooting.

"Get moving," barked Raider. "And chrissakes keep your heads down! And spread out."

"The grass is good cover," began Donahue, his hand on the latch, preparing to open the door.

"For ground birds and bugs," said Raider sardonically. "Give me rocks and trees any day."

"What are *you* going to do?" George asked.

"Good question." Raider looked about him. "Hide someplace, if I can."

"There's a cold cellar," offered Donahue. He indicated the pile of driftwood alongside the stove. "Underneath there. The cellar's empty and it's big enough, but its damp as hell. They wouldn't see the trapdoor if we piled wood on top of it."

Raider lowered himself into the cold cellar, detailing strategy off the top of his head as he scrunched down. The hole was cramped and shallow, and even colder than Donahue had intimated, but made for a good hideout, providing he didn't have to stay there all night. He pulled the door down, plunging the hole into pitch darkness. They piled firewood on top of it.

"Just enough to cover it," he cautioned, calling upward. "If it's too heavy I'll never be able to push it up."

He heard the piling of the wood stop. Their heavy feet pounded the floor, setting the boards creaking protestingly. The door closed and all was quiet. A troubling thought crossed his mind. Was it possible he and Doc had led the assassination squad to Mandeville? Had they followed them down the road to the hideout? Any one of the seven other passengers on the train to Slidell could have been on their tail, even the twelve-year-old with his mother and father.

What difference did it make how they'd found the place? They were here, that was all that mattered. How many? he wondered. Six, ten, fifteen? Not that many.

Would that Donahue would use his head for a change and follow instructions. He would if George kept on his ear. They would join Forzaglia, then all three withdraw, pulling the mobsters back to within a hundred yards of the place. Then, if they did as he'd told them, the two of them and "Officer" Provenzano would split up, each one covering a side of the house and the rear, leaving the visitors clear access to the front. Hopefully, they would charge the place, bust in, and begin tearing everything apart, looking for him.

"Son of a bitch!" In his haste to formulate some kind of defense strategy, get Donahue and George out to join Forzaglia, and himself down into the cold cellar, he had completely overlooked his disguise.

"Screw it, what the hell good would it do face to face anyhow?"

A conversation he had had with Doc years before came back to him. They had been on their way to San Francisco, the train girdling the Wasatch Range. Doc had his nose in a book as usual, *The Fall of Troy* or *Troy Falls*, something. He told him about the wooden horse, how the Greeks filled it with soldiers and when the Trojans opened their gates and rolled it inside, that night the soldiers got out and opened the gates and let in the rest of the Greeks, and that finished Troy.

Squatting in the darkness, he eased from side to side, his shoulders touching the walls. This was *his* wooden horse, sort of, he mused. They'd come storming in and start tearing the place apart looking for him, George. When they didn't find him, they'd sit down and start talking what to do next. That would be his cue. He'd jump up and start blasting.

It sounded so simple. It was anything but. What if there were six or seven, even more? He had six shots; each one would have to kill instantly. Lift the door with one hand and jump up firing with the other. Like a jack-in-the-box. Reaching upward, he tested the door with both hands. It moved easily, but he hesitated to lift it too high for fear the wood would roll off, exposing it.

Sequence: Push up, slam open, jump up shooting, shooting, shooting. One step at a time, all in order, consuming five, possibly six seconds. And what would they be doing in the meantime? Watching, cheering, applauding? It would take them all of two seconds to react. And what if somebody was behind him. They could stamp down on the door before he could raise it two inches. Stamp it down, stand on it, and fill it with more holes than a damn sieve!

Cocking one ear, he waited. Not a sound, not even the wind murmuring. His thoughts drifted to George and the two cops. A shoot-out in that grass would be murder. There was nothing solid for any kind of cover—no horse trough, no shed corners, no trees, rocks. Even down flat, squirming along on your belly, you maybe couldn't be seen, but the grass above you could. And the moon was almost full.

What if they got all three of them, even George? Outgunned and surrounded, they could easily. Kill all three, close ranks, march up to the house, bust the windows, stuff the holes with grass, and burn the place to the ground. Easy as toasting an ear of corn. If he showed his face, they'd blow him in half. If he stayed where he was, he'd smother to death with smoke.

"Some stinking grave this is. Doesn't even fit, for chris-sakes!"

His knees had begun aching furiously. He quit his crouch, lowering into a kneeling position, as if preparing to pray, he thought grimly. He had to keep some strength, some spring in his knees for when it came time to jump upward. If he ever got the chance. Raising the trapdoor slightly, he listened. He could hear sporadic gunfire, but was unable to pinpoint the exact location. He estimated he had been down in the cellar at least twenty minutes before the firing ceased. And did not resume.

Was that good news or bad, he wondered? Any moment now, either attackers or defenders would come through the door. If his hastily formulated plan worked, the mobsters would be coming in and George and the two cops would be positioned on three sides of the place, lying in the grass watching. Once whoever was covering the sides saw them approaching the door, the play would be for all three to circle around behind them. He himself would jump up and start blasting. Common sense figured they would turn around and run back out, straight into the cop's guns. Common sense? More like luck.

He waited, pondering the situation, sniffling in the dampness of his hole, repositioning himself on his haunches in a vain effort to ease the strain, and wincing as both knees began throbbing dully. He got out his six-gun and set his free hand against the trapdoor. And listened intently. He counted to a hundred and was approaching a hundred and forty when the outside door flew open. They came stomping in. A jumble of feet; he could not make out how many. Chair legs scraped the floor; the table was moved. He tensed, preparing to jump out, then caught himself.

"Sit there, cop. Move, and I'll shoot your goddamn face off! Understand?"

Raider's heart sank like a rock. More chairs pushed about. The door was slammed, the bolt thrown. The two bedroom doors were opened and closed in turn.

"Nobody here, Vito," said a high-pitched voice.

"Sit down and shut up. What's your name, cop? You Italian?"

"Greek."

Raider swallowed. It was George. No mistaking that peculiar, muscle-locked, slightly strained tone. He sounded surprisingly calm, almost relaxed. Forzaglia and Donahue were no doubt lying somewhere out in the grass full of holes, but he had been spared. For a time, at least. Ironically, if not incredibly, they failed to recognize him. Bless your brains, Weatherbee, he mused; sometimes your ideas are polished gemstones.

"You look Italian," said the man giving the orders. "What's your name?"

"Stavros Karisopolis."

"Okay, Karis—"

"—opolis."

"You're the only one left. You seen what happened to your two partners." There came the ominous sound of a gun being cocked. "I don't like cops. They're nothing but trouble. But you're not gonna give us no trouble, are you? You're gonna help us. You help us, you tell us what we want, and you don't get a bullet in your head."

"In your belly," said another voice and guffawed raucously.

"Shut up!" snapped the man in charge. "I'm gonna ask you a question, Karis. Answer me right and you got nothing to worry about. You can get up and walk right out the door. Right, boys?"

"Sure, we wouldn't want to hurt you none."

Snickering, and again a reprimand from the man addressing George.

"We're looking for the *paisan* you were guarding, George Provenzano. Where is he?"

"Never heard of him."

Raider tensed. The gun going off in the small room sounded like a cannon fired into a barrel. Pain pounded his eardrums like twin knife points stabbing deep.

"That was close, Karis, I almost clipped your ear."

Raider sighed, sucked a tooth, filled his lungs with the damp, stale air, raised his hand once more, setting it flat against the trapdoor, lifted his Peacemaker muzzle upward, and shoved. Up he sprang, drilling one shot into the temple of the man sitting opposite George, waving his gun at him. Three others stood about. Raider got one going for his shoulder holster, but the second one got his gun out and pumping. A slug slammed into Raider's shoulder; a second got him in the right chest, ramming him against the back of the trapdoor opening, all but snapping his spine. He returned fire, his first shot plowing into the other's heart.

Number three was aiming. Vaulting from his chair head down, George butted him in the shoulder, forcing his outstretched arm to one side, spoiling his aim, the shot going wild, splintering the floor. George seized the table, swinging it laterally, the edge of it catching the man full in the throat; the sound of cartilege crunching, a stifled outcry, and he collapsed in a heap.

Raider lay against the back of the hole, gaping at the ceiling, his front drenched with blood. George came quickly to him.

"I got you . . . Take it easy."

Raider's mouth was filling with blood—warm, salty. He tried to respond, but it spewed forth uncontrollably like vomit. The room whirled, canted, dissolved. He passed out.

CHAPTER FIFTEEN

Four hours later Raider lay in a bed in Room 204 of Charity Hospital on Tulane Avenue in the heart of the city. The slug had been extracted from his shoulder, but he had lost so much blood the doctor hesitated to go into his chest in quest of the second slug.

George Provenzano had saved his life. To prevent any interference from the sole surviving member of the trio, the man he had struck with the table, he had put a bullet through his head. He stopped Raider's copious bleeding, carried him to the canoe at the dock, and paddled across the lake to New Orleans. Arriving, he had gotten hold of a doctor and arrangements were speedily made to transport the patient to the hospital. George then sent word to the Hotel Gregg, demanding that Doc come to the hospital immediately.

The two of them stood outside Raider's door, talking in low tones, George still in his uniform, his face gray with weariness, barely able to get his words out, so exhausted was he. But, noted Doc, his loyalty to the cause was continuing as staunch as ever—if anything, reinforced by the harrowing and bloody episode of the night before. Bright sunlight slanted through the window behind George, patching the floor, creating a gleaming platform where he stood. Appraising him as he listened to him, it occurred to Doc that the light should be collecting about the big man's head, forming a halo. Raider owed him his life; they both owed him a bargeload of gratitude for his immense contribution to the case; Mayor Shakespeare, District Attorney Luzenberg, every official in town and every law-abiding citizen was in his debt. Most pleasing of all to Doc was that George had become almost fanatical in his commitment to the case, in his determination to see it through to its conclusion. To hammer home the last nail in the mob's coffin.

"We've got to find someplace where you can hole up for the next few days," said Doc. "Maybe you should move around, a few days here, a few there. You shouldn't be staying in town."

"I was thinking about that, paddling across the lake last night. Isn't that what they'd figure, that I'd keep away from town? But look at me." He took a step backward, spreading his arms, then rubbing his chin. "Do I look like me? Those bastards up at the lake didn't spot me. Not even up close. The fat one doing all the talking was sitting across the table *asking me where I was hiding out*, can you imagine? If I hadn'ta been so scared I'da laughed in his face. Doc, I'm in the best disguise there is!"

"Good point." He snapped his fingers. "I've got it. Button up, spruce up, maybe shave."

"And report for duty at the Central Police Station." He grinned and saluted. "Officer Stavros Karisopolis reporting for duty."

"Who?"

"That's a name I made up out at the lake when the fat guy had me on the pan, you know? Stavros Karisopolis."

"Maybe I should go with you, Stavros. We can talk things over with Montaigne. On second thought, I wouldn't want to stretch our luck too far."

"What's to stretch? We're both cops, we can be seen together."

"I think it's better you see him alone. Introduce yourself. I mean he certainly won't recognize you when you walk in. Fill him in on last night. Tell him I'm sticking around here. Get him to give you some kind of desk job, something that'll keep you inside, okay? Maybe a job where you'll be off by yourself. And whatever you do, stay away from the cells. Somebody might spot you."

"Nobody will. Last night was the big test, and I passed easy, you know?"

"What if they bring Joe in?"

George's face darkened. "Yeah... Don't worry, I'll be careful, I kinda like living. When we get this thing all cleaned up I'm gonna start!"

Again he saluted smartly and started down the corridor. Doc eased Raider's door open and went in. One look and he blanched, drawing his breath in sharply. Raider resembled a corpse; the suggestion traversing Doc's mind made him wince. Raider's cheeks were almost as pale as the top sheet drawn up to his chin. Doc set a chair alongside the bed.

"Rade, can you hear me? Don't try to talk. Don't say anything, just answer with your eyes. Blink for yes; for no, don't move your eyelids at all." He leaned closer. "Can you hear me?"

Blink.

"When you were crouching down in the cold cellar you could hear them, right?"

Blink.

"Did anybody say anything that might help? Mention any names?"

Nothing.

"Maybe talk about a job?"

Nothing.

The door opened. Under a bush of flaming red hair the doctor's features were florid, his expression irate.

"Who are you? What do you think you're doing in here?"

"This man is my partner."

"He's *my* patient. He's in no condition to talk."

"He's not; he's just answering a few questions by blinking his eyes."

"He's barely conscious; he's loaded with morphine. Whatever it is you want to know will have to wait."

Doc nodded and stood up. "How is he doing?"

"If he was any worse he'd be dead. He's so low on blood

I'm leery about operating. But I've got to. The longer I wait, the worse his chances. He's got a bullet in his lung. It's got to come out."

"He's very strong, he has extraordinary stamina."

"I can see that. Nine out of ten never would have made it across the lake. He's tough as a pine knot, only he's not pine, he's flesh and blood, and right now he's hanging on by a thread. The last thing he needs is visitors. Beat it."

"Of course."

The doctor followed him out. He altered his tone. "I'm sorry, I didn't mean to be rude, but he's in rotten shape. Strong as he is, he may not make it. Frankly, I'll be amazed if he does."

"Isn't there something you can do for him?"

"That's a fairly dumb question, mister! If there was, don't you think I'd be doing it? What do you suggest, I wave a magic wand over him? I've penciled him in for two o'clock this afternoon. Cross your fingers." He studied Doc's eyes. "You a religious man?"

"Not very."

"Try a little; pray for him." He held his hands up, looking from one to the other. "For me, too, while you're at it." He was standing opposite him, the bed between them. "You two are partners, you said. In what?"

"The lumber business."

"What was he doing, swiping somebody else's trees? There's no lumber across the lake. Never mind, it's none of my business."

"When can I see him again?"

"After he's operated on he'll go to the recovery room. How long he stays there depends more on bed availability than anything else. Come back around five and check. If everything goes well he could be back here by then. We're a little cramped for space around here; we generally leave patients in the recovery room just about long enough to come out of the anesthesia." He smiled. "If they can wet their lips they're classified as recovered. I may be giving you the idea this place is more like a meat-packing plant than a hospital. It is, but we do our best. Five o'clock."

"Thank you."

"That door down at the end leads to the stairs that go down directly to the street."

Doc started off, stopped, and turned to look back. "There'll be a couple of policemen coming to guard his door."

The doctor grinned. "Dangerous doings, the lumber business."

News of Raider's encounter with the two .44 slugs had visibly upset Frank Montaigne. He and Doc sat talking in his office, Doc describing Raider's condition, optimistically evaluating his chances. He was trying his best to sound optimistic, but feeling anything but in his heart.

"Every time you turn around somebody else is getting it," complained Montaigne. "Bullet in the lung is rough. You really think he'll make it?"

"I'm hoping and praying."

"He's one tough son of a gun, scrap iron wrapped round with barbed wire. I bet you two been through some rough scrapes togethah. He's probably been shot at with everything that loads, isn't that so?"

"Just about. You should see him in his skin." Doc explored his own body with his fingertips. "He's got so many holes and scars, bumps, slashes. He looks like somebody pushed him through a revolving grater then finished the job with hammer and chisel. And his insides; I'm sure his liver is where his gall bladder should be and most of everything else has relocated."

"You two been pahtners a long time?"

"A hundred and fifty years or so."

Montaigne shook his head, his expression wonderment. "You'ah so different, everything about you, everything. How in the world do you get togethah? How do you see eye to eye on anything?"

"Generally, we don't. That's what makes it interesting."

"I bet you've had *some* knock-down, drag-out set-tos."

"You name it, we've argued about it, toe to toe. Damn it all, he's got to make it! Got to! You work with somebody as long as we've worked and you reach a point where you simply take it for granted it's going to go on and on. Forever. Time does that, you know—gives you a false sense of invincibility. The longer the time, the more confident you become. It's like your reward for coming through the wars, for surviving, is immortality. You really begin to believe that's so. When it's the two of you against six or seven of them and you wipe them out, you win again, it reinforces your conviction that the merry-go-round's never going to stop. Self-deception is an enticing state of mind. Also stupid."

"It's not."

"It's human nature, I know."

"I'll light a candle foh him," said Montaigne. "That'll help." He laid a reassuring hand on Doc's knee. "Listen, I got something else that'll help, some good news you can give him when you go back."

"I almost forgot, did George Provenzano show up here?"

Montaigne nodded. "I gave him pad and pencil and a room to himself. He plans to spend all day scouring his memory. Also, Captain O'Conner's been badgering ouah friend Enzo and it's finally paid off. He's dictated and signed a statement admitting he fingahed the chief and implicating the two othahs. And that's not all. We got two moah prisoners talking."

"Sounds like the rats are deserting the sinking ship."

Montaigne beamed and rubbed his hands together briskly. "I'm getting to feel bettah and bettah about the whole mess." He indicated the calendar hanging alongside the clock above his desk. "Grand jury meets Thursday. Everything we've got is in the D.A.'s hands now, everything except George's memoirs. And we'll get his infohmation ovah to Luzenberg soon as he's done getting it all down. The mayor's been riding my back like a jockey on a horse. The jury's already impaneled. Luzenberg'll throw everything he's got in theah laps, and parade all the witnesses by 'em." He chuckled. "All foah, that's all we got at the moment. Provenzano, Enzo, and the othah two back in the cells. Course five, really. You'll be testifying."

"All I can tell them about is the Council meeting."

"It'll help. More colors we can get into the picture, the brighter it'll be, right? Meantime, we'ah rounding up the othahs that were at the meeting that night, all we can find, including brothah Joe. The two Provenzanos'll be eyeballing each othah even befoah the trial. That should be something to see. What we got to get us is what they call a 'true bill.' Ouah ticket to an indictment. Then comes the arraignment. It's looking good, Doc. Bettah and bettah." he paused. "You want to look in on old George? Man sure does look a sight different clean-shaved. He walked in heah I didn't recognize him foh souah apples." He got up. "Come along, I'll walk you ovah theah."

"Not now, Frank. No point in my disturbing his train of thought." He paused. "He thinks he's safe here at the station. What do you think?"

"I doubt anybody'll recognize him. I'm not going to let him wandah the halls, if that's what's worrying you. One thing working foh him: Theah's nothing unusual about a strange face showing up heah. Unifohms from all ovah town come and go all the time. The regulah boys'll just take it foh granted he's from anothah precinct."

Doc said good-bye and went back to the hotel to nap for a couple of hours in anticipation of an all-night vigil by Raider's bedside. He awoke a little after two o'clock. He walked to the river and took the free ferry across to Gretna, planning to look in on Billy Cobb. His conscience urged him to bring her up to date. She was entitled to know what had happened to Raider. He located the house and introduced himself to her landlady, according the woman the benefit of doubt as to whether or not she was successor to Emma Pickett. He was told that Billy had gone out. He left a note saying he'd be back at ten the next morning, adding that he had news "concerning a mutual friend." He signed the note "Mr. Hastings."

He returned to Charity Hospital at five sharp, crossing his fingers as he mounted the front steps, his heart thumping nervously. Frank Montaigne had described Raider colorfully, calling him scrap iron wrapped in barbed wire. Would that he were scrap iron, mused Doc, worriedly; so the doctor could extract the bullet with a magnet without losing one more drop of his so precious and so dangerously depleted blood supply.

The receptionist's spectacles magnified her eyes to nearly twice normal size. Set deep in her pudgy, flabby, disagreeable face, they glared suspiciously at him. He tipped his hat cordially and murmured greeting. She grunted. All sweetness, light, and personality, he thought to himself.

"Mr. O'Toole, please."

"What number?"

"Mr.—"

"We go by patient's room numbers, not names. Shall we start over again?"

"Two-oh-four."

"Before you answer, I ask; do you understand? We have procedures here and we prefer to follow them. Let's begin again. What number?"

"Two-oh-four."

She consulted a clipboard, riffling through pages with fingers that resembled knuckled ladyfinger cookies minus their powdered sugar. She checked, she double-checked.

"Two-oh-four. O'Toole."

"That's right. He was operated on this aft—"

"You a relative?"

"I... What's that got to do... I mean..." He caught his irritation, clamping it down securely, modulating his tone. "The doctor told me to come back at five. It's now two minutes past. He may not be back in his room yet."

"He's not going back. He's downstairs in the cooler."

"WHAT!"

"Don't shout. This is a hospital, you're not to raise your voice. I'm sorry, but Mr. O'Toole is dead."

"That's impossible," he blurted out. "He can't be!"

"See for yourself." She held up the clipboard, indicating the room number, the name O'Toole, J., then moved her pencil to the right to a capital D.

"'D,' what do you think that stands for? Deceased, that's what. Deceased, that means dead." Leaning forward, crushing her massive breasts against the edge of the desk, she pointed down the corridor. "See that door to the left? Go through it and down the stairs. The attendant on duty will show you the body."

CHAPTER SIXTEEN

The morgue was cold in the manner of a cellar, only clammier, which attribute Doc chalked up to his nerves. On his way down the stairs he began to feel nauseous. Coming up to the door, he peered through the wire-webbed glass. The chair behind the little table to the right was empty. He glanced up and down the dimly lit corridor.

"Hello..."

The word echoed back to him. He went in. Whoever was in charge had evidently stepped out for a smoke. The "No Smoking" sign on the far wall suggested it. No reason for him not to duck out, reflected Doc, he needn't worry about any of his charges wandering off.

He glanced down the lines of wooden vaults stacked three high on either side, seventy-two in all. They were numbered, the first stack to his left, 1A, top, 2A, center, 3A, bottom. The table top was bare. There was a drawer; he was tempted to open it, reasoning that there had to be an identification list of some sort and the drawer seemed the likeliest place to keep it. But the drawer had a lock.

He took a deep breath and moved to 2A, abruptly seized by the urge to pull it open and check the identity of the occupant. His hand went to the grip, but then let go of it, his eyes drifting back to the "No Smoking" sign, for no reason but to give them something to do. He sat at the little table, his derby off, drumming the top of it with his fingers, and waited. He still felt sick to his stomach, like a small boy who had eaten too much cotton candy, he thought. But worse than that, far worse, was the crushing sensation of loss slowly taking possession of him. As he sat there, he imagined an unseen assailant skillfully and methodically cutting his heart out. And he refused to budge, letting him dig and slice at will.

Raider dead.

It couldn't be. It was impossible. It hadn't happened. Oh, it was a risky operation, no question, but he'd *never* die on any operating table. Any more than he'd die in bed.

He closed his eyes and onto the screen of his imagination came that grouchy face, lean and lined and weathered like an old boot, the dark, piercing eyes, the gleaming white teeth, the false one he himself had purchased for him after knocking the real one down his throat. What had that fight been about, anyway? He searched his memory, but couldn't recall. There'd been so many fights.

He lay spread-eagled on the slab onto which the force of the slug had flipped him, too exhausted to even stir his legs. It began to rain, a gentle patter bobbing the heads of the Indian paintbrush, standing in a clump of grass at the edge of the slab. Striking Raider's eyes, his cheeks, his wounds. He had lost a great deal of blood, was still losing it. It oozed out of his wounds, taking his strength with it. Opening his mouth, he caught raindrops, tasting their cool sweetness, sending a slender rivulet down his parched throat.

He thought of death. He had been shot before any number of times. Badly, dangerously wounded. In action the thought of death had flashed across his mind and lay the stone egg of fear in the pit of his stomach, tightening the cords at the back of his neck, driving sweat out of him faster and more profusely. But that was sudden death, easy death. This was creeping death, venturing nearer and nearer like a curious snake, approaching where he lay, circling him, studying him from every angle, pronouncing him right and ready to be taken.

"Rade, Rade..."

He saw himself lying in bed in Dr. Finegan's upstairs office in Leslie, a pinprick on the map of Colorado, the sheet up to his chin, feeling, sensing, knowing without question that he had come so close to the black shadow it could reach out and touch him, capture him, wrap him in its folds. Dr. Finegan had taken four bullets out of him, and he had awakened to find himself stripped to the waist, his chest and shoulders strapped in an ascending spica bandage. He was so weak and exhausted he could scarcely get air into his lungs. The doctor was standing at the foot of the bed; Raider was sitting alongside, giving him hell for getting himself shot up, decrying his carelessness, ridiculing his tactics. His customary way of unburdening himself of sympathy: insults, abuse, gibes, and jeers. Finegan listened, staring in disbelief.

"This man was at death's door!"

"Oh, horseshit! He's hardly scratched, for chrissakes. You wanta see real wounds? I'll show you some. How the hell long you gonna lay there, Doc? Time's a-fleeting. Take 'bout fifteen minutes more, better ten, then get up and get your fancy duds on. We gotta long ride ahead o' us."

There was always death talk in the business, opinions, conjecture. Many men he knew firmly believed that death's visitation was recognizable, not merely through assumption, but by virtue of certain very definite indicators. For example, the languor that settled over one, the onset of the temptation to give in, the overwhelming exhaustion rendering it impossible, even foolish, to refuse, a sensation of softness, of invisible clouds enveloping one, wrapping you in their folds, slipping underneath you. And buoying you upward. And any pain dissipated little by little with the coming of the cloud, eventually vanishing altogether.

No pain, no feelings whatsoever, no cold, no heat. It was, he had heard, as if one's body from the neck down dissolved into a mist to be swept away by the breeze.

What would he do without a Raider in his life? How could he function alone, or with another operative—some stranger thrown at him by Wagner and Allan Pinkerton? No! He'd rather quit. He'd had his fill of the business. Almost fifteen years.

He was still a young man, comparatively, not yet forty. There must be something else he could do with what was left of his life. Only what?

The door opened. A young, round-shouldered, slack-jawed man came dragging in, smelling of tobacco. He wore hospital whites, even to his shoes; his tunic was buttoned up one shoulder. He seemed surprised at the sight of Doc. Doc rose from his chair.

"Hi-yah," said the attendant good-naturedly. "Sorry to keep you waiting. Had to check on something. What's the name?"

"John O'Toole."

The attendant nodded, obviously recognizing it. He motioned Doc to follow him down the line of vaults on the right, pausing before the twenty-fours, pulling open 24B. The body was wrapped in a sheet. They stood on either side. The attendant turned down the sheet, revealing the corpse's face. Doc swallowed and scowled.

"That's not him."

"John O'Toole," the attendant insisted.

He pulled the drawer out as far as it would go. The tag on the big toe read "John O'Toole."

"What'd I tell you?"

"I'm telling you it's not him! This is the wrong drawer. It's got to be."

"That's impossible. Only one stiff come down this afternoon. I know, I been on since noon. I checked him in. That's my handwriting on the tag."

"Something's screwed up."

"It can't be, I'm telling you."

Doc walked off, muttering. Then he broke into a run, leaving the door open behind him. He raced down the corridor and up the stairs to reception. Huge-eyes was still at her desk, writing, her fat lips forming words. He ran up to her.

"Excuse me . . ."

"One moment, please. As you can see I'm busy."

"Where's the doctor?" He reached over, flattening his hand against the paper she was writing on, rendering it impossible for her to continue. She jerked up her head, glaring pitchforks.

"Take your hand off that paper or I'll stick this pen straight through it! Doctor who?"

"I don't know his name. The one with the bushy red hair. The one who operated on O'Toole."

"Dr. Knowles. He's probably in the doctors' lounge. He may even be in surgery."

"You don't know, is that it?"

"Keep your voice down!"

A doctor and nurse came by. Doc spun about, confronting them. "Do either of you know where Dr. Knowles is?"

They exchanged glances. The doctor shook his head. The nurse thought a moment.

"The last I saw of him was up on the second floor. He was looking in on a patient. Two-ten? Yes, two-ten."

Doc blurted thanks and ran off with the receptionist screaming after him.

"Wait a minute, you can't go up without a pass. You hear me?"

He heard her, he ignored her. He found 210 and burst in. Raider lay supported by two pillows, eyes open, pale as his support. He looked twenty pounds lighter, his face hanging from his skull, his cheeks cavernous. Dr. Knowles was checking his pulse.

"Rade, Rade, Rade, God in heaven!"

The explanation for the mix-up was logical, if not simple. Raider had been taken from 204 upstairs to pre-op. He had gone under the scalpel at two o'clock, according to Knowles. The operation completed, he had been removed to the recovery room. While this sequence was unfolding, another patient, a man suffering from advanced heart disease, sharing a room with three other patients, had been transferred to 204. For no reason, assumed and explained Dr. Knowles, but to permit him to die in privacy. Evidently, a few minutes after taking occupancy of 204, he had obliged. His doctor, doubtless temporarily overburdened with other duties, neglected to notify the desk downstairs that he had ordered his patient moved to 204. As far as the receptionist was concerned, Patient O'Toole in 204 had gone into surgery, had come out of surgery, had been returned to his room, quietly passed away, and his remains were removed to the morgue.

"I'll give you three minutes," said Knowles, eyeing his watch.

"He's weak as a kitten. He's not to say one word, is that understood? Any questions you want him to answer, he can blink."

"No questions," said Doc.

"What do you mean, 'no questions'? This morning you were practically ready to rip my head off."

"A lot has happened since. Everything's changed. With your permission, I just want to stand here and look at him. He's going to be okay, right?"

"He is with that slug out of him."

"Wonderful! You hear that, Rade? You're going to be fine." Raider grunted.

"Don't grunt!" snapped the doctor. "Not a sound out of you, I mean it." He turned to Doc, fish-eyeing him. "Whatever happened to the two policemen you were going to get to stand guard outside?"

Doc caught himself, frowning. "Good Lord. Do you know I completely forgot to even mention it to Frank? With everything that's been happening... So much at once..."

"Asshole," muttered Raider weakly.

The doctor moved to him quickly, hovering over him. "I said no talking, damn it! I know you're three-quarters brontosaurus, but you can still relapse."

"Mmmm."

"Not even that. All we need is for you to start bleeding internally."

"Rade, I'll leave you alone. I've a lot to tell you, but nothing that can't wait. Billy's okay; Frank, George, everybody. I've got nothing but good news, the best. This is one we're going to win with you flat on your back."

Raider said nothing, casting his eyes at the doctor warily. Then he locked a withering scowl of disapproval on his face and directed it at his partner.

CHAPTER SEVENTEEN

While Raider lay on Dr. Knowles's operating table in Charity Hospital, Chief David Hennessey was solemnly eulogized and his remains interred, the ceremony attended by thousands of citizens, prominent and little known, friends and strangers. In the hysterical atmosphere surrounding the assassination, Mayor Shakespeare was quoted as saying, "We must teach these people a lesson they will not forget for all time."

Lieutenant Montaigne spread his net over the city, catching "fish" of every size, description, and rank in the Mafia. Among his prizes were Joe Macia, head of the Macia Steamship line; Charles Matranga, known to the city as "Millionaire Charlie"; Joe Provenzano, the banana king; and Rocco Gerace, a wealthy businessman who reputedly controlled nearly half the bordellos in town. Racial disturbances came on the heels of the roundup. Anyone who even looked Italian, anyone with an accent suspected of being Italian locked his doors and windows, pulled down the shades, and waited for the hysteria to abate. District Attorney Luzenberg was to go before the grand jury with his evidence and witnesses in quest of a true bill. While the prisoners languished in Old Parish Prison, the eighteen-year-old son of a prominent New Orleans businessman slipped into the prison and shot Adolfo Orsini, one of the accused.

"I'm willing to hang if one of those Dagos dies, and I wish there were seventy-five men more like me," the killer told the guards who apprehended him.

The prevailing sentiment infecting the city was reflected in the New Orleans *Times-Democrat* headline of Tuesday evening: "Assassination Attempt of One of the Accused Dagos."

Giuseppe Esposito and Tony Matranga successfully evaded Lieutenant Montaigne's net and were still at large. It was rumored that both were still in the city on Thursday, the day the grand jury was to hear District Attorney Luzenberg's case against the Mafia. The grand jury concentrated on one specific crime only, Chief Hennessey's murder. The hearing was closed to the public, but outside the building hundreds of reporters from all over the South and thousands of curious citizens waited for the outcome of the proceedings.

Shortly before six in the evening, the doors opened and Thomas Freeling, an associate of Luzenberg's, called for silence and formally announced the grand jury's decision. The crowd roared approval. Nineteen of the prisoners were indicted, eleven as principals and eight as accessories to Hennessey's murder.

The case would go to trial.

Doc met George Provenzano on the way out and together they went to a restaurant in the French Quarter for brisket of beef with horseradish sauce. Doc was jubilant over the outcome of the proceedings, but George appeared somewhat subdued. Doc did not need to ask why.

"I can't wait for tomorrow morning," Doc said. "Wait'll Raider hears the good news. I'd run over there now, only they don't allow visitors after six. Crazy rules."

"Did you see his face?"

"Joe's?"

George nodded. "He looked like death." He paused and made the sign of the cross. "All the fight drained outta him. He looked like somebody'd kicked the wind outta him, no spirit left, no heart. He had tears in his eyes, did you see?"

"Yes. I was watching him when Luzenberg was examining you. He couldn't take his eyes off you."

"I know, I saw, that's why I kept my head down. I just couldn't look at him. I swear to God, it's enough to bust your heart in your chest."

"He didn't look bitter, George, there was no hatred. His expression wasn't vicious like the others. I know, I was watching him like a hawk."

"How could he look bitter, for chrissakes? He's stunned, in shock!" He shook his head discouragedly, his elbow on the table, one hand propping up his forehead. "I don't understand."

He paused to look up. The waiter was accosting them, waving menus, a slightly built, bilious-looking man in shirt-sleeves with a black bow tie supporting his prominent Adam's apple.

"Something to drink, gennemen?"

"Bring us a bottle o' Chianti. Okay?" George looked to Doc for approval and got a nod. "Beef and Chianti go good, you know?"

"What don't you understand?" Doc asked.

"Joe. He knew all along it was coming. He knew I'd be, you know, testifying. How come he looked so shocked?"

"He knew it was coming, but he probably tried to tell himself it was just a threat, a shadow on the horizon. It would never come to pass. It was a ticking bomb, but it would never explode. Nothing would come of it. In time it would all just fade away. He can't believe it's actually happening. He probably sat there pinching himself."

"I gotta go see him."

"At the prison?"

"That's where he is, isn't he?" He glared accusingly.

"You think that's wise?"

"He's my brother! I got to. Christ, I owe him that much. Besides, he's got nobody else—no wife, no kids, only his loyal, loving brother."

The wine arrived. He snatched up the bottle, pouring so hastily he spilled a little. He emptied his glass with one swig and refilled it.

"Who ratted on him."

"That really bothers you, doesn't it?"

"What do you think?"

"It's in your belly. You've let it in. Are you going to let it eat at you from now on?"

"I guess it depends on what happens to him. How bad. If they hang him, you bet it'll eat at me from now on. If they give him life, I'll be in prison too. This prison." He released the glass, gesturing, his hands on either side of his massive head. *"Capish?"*

"That's stupid." The words came out as flat, as cold, as devoid of feeling as he could make them.

"Hey, cop, don't go starting up with me."

"Stupid. Dumb. At this late date, after all we've been through, you still can't get it through your skull. You're doing the only thing you can do, the right thing. Doing it because you have to. It's not nearly as complicated as you seem determined to make it. Simply stated, you happen to be in a position to help the state, to do what is right. And you're doing it. For the city, for your family, for yourself. For Peter. Damn it, even for Joe!"

George drank again without tasting the wine, more to give his hands something to do than in response to thirst. "I'm putting a rope around my own brother's neck."

"Do you want to retract your statement?"

"You think what I did in that chair today, you think raising my right hand to God and answering them questions with all o' them sitting there staring daggers at me, you think that was easy?"

"Of course it wasn't. It was hell on earth, the hardest thing you've ever done. Given a choice, you'd rather cut off your right hand. But, that's the problem, George, there is no choice."

"You know something? You know what'd help. If, after it's all over—the trial, the whole works—and he knows what his sentence is gonna be, if him and me could sit down and he could look me in the eye, like I'm looking at you, and say, Georgie, it's all over and now I can say it. Georgie, I honest to God got no hard feelings. I forgive you. You had to do what you thought was right, and it was, and you done it and I forgive you. That would help, you know, Doc? Oh, Jesus, Mary, and Joseph, it would help so much!"

"Want to bet that's exactly what he'll do? Not just for you, for him, for his conscience. For his soul, George."

"He'll never, not in ten million years. He's stubborn as hell, what we call *ostinato*."

"Obstinate. I still bet he will."

"I'm gonna ask him straight out when I go see him tonight. That's if he'll even see me. He could refuse. He probably will."

"You said before you'd wait till it's all over. You should. You're right when you say he's in shock. Give him time to come out of it. When it's all over, when he's accepted the verdict, when he realizes he's going to have to live with it, I bet he'll forgive you without your even asking him."

"That's a sucker bet. Don't bet nothing. Just cross your fingers for me. Come on, let's order. I'm starving."

Raider was recovering "splendidly"—Dr. Knowles's word. The patient himself was somewhat less sanguine over his condition. He did not consider himself "halfway through death's door," only within reach of the knocker. Doc's daily visits and his good news bulletins failed to lift his spirits. Knowing his partner as Doc did, this came as neither a surprise nor a disappointment. He often wondered if he was deliberately courting hardening of the arteries, consuming such an abundance of salt, taking as he did every other statement of Raider's with a grain of it.

"I'll never be able to breathe right again, I just know it. No more high country riding, where the air thins out, either. I'm gonna have to watch out for colds and sneezing and things like that the rest o' my days. The littlest nose drip could turn into pee-neumonia. God forbid I ever catch another slug in the chest. I could get the consumption easier than you can shake a stick, and have to spend the rest o' my days in one of those consumption hospitals, spitting into basins all day. I'm gonna be six months getting back all the blood I spilled. Goddamn hole."

"In your chest?"

"In the floor, for chrissakes! It was so cramped I couldn't get my iron up and working; banged my hand against the side o' the trap. Bastard never woulda got *a* shot off, let alone two. I coulda wiped out all three, one second each if I hadn'ta been cramped in so. Look at me, helpless as a kitten. Your partner's a invalid, Weatherbee, full-fledged, good for nothing and nobody. The old man'll turn me out to pasture for sure. I'll likely end up sitting on some street corner, my Stetson in my lap, peddling pencils."

"You're not blind, Rade. Can you turn off your whiner for a little bit? Things have been happening you should know about."

"The trial. I know. You and Montaigne and that D.A. fella think you're home free, don't you? You're gonna get some surprise, you are. The Mafia got more money than the U.S. mint. They're gonna be buying off everybody walks through the door—judge, jury, witnesses, everybody 'cept the janitor. When the lying and the bullshitting and falsifying start flying round that courtroom, God and all the angels upstairs are gonna have to stuff cotton in their ears."

"Luzenberg knows that, Rade, but let me tell you something—something you know all too well from experience. When things are going good, you know how it is, how a little seed of suspicion plants itself, a warning that you're coming to a corner, things are going to start going sour. And vice versa, right? Things are going good for us. We may very well come to that corner, but I don't feel it. I'm up to my ears in confidence. We all are, even the two pessimists, Montaigne and Luzenberg. Everything's falling into place exactly as we want. I'm telling you the Mafia in New Orleans is finished."

The door opened. Dr. Knowles stood clutching his stethoscope, grinning. "How's the the world's champion combination hypochondriac-grouch today?"

"He's great!" burst out Doc. "Tell him, Rade."

Raider grunted.

"Any discomfort?"

Raider drew his hand across his chest. "It's sore like a bruise."

"That's normal. Guess what? You're going ambulatory today."

"Great!" exclaimed Doc. "That means you're going to get out of bed and walk, Rade."

"No can do. I'm too friggin' weak."

Knowles laughed. "You could beat the two of us to a pulp in ninety seconds, that's how 'weak' you are." He pulled back the covers, revealing the hem of Raider's Johnny shirt and his gnarled and slightly bowed legs. "On your feet."

Raider glared, but did as he was told, standing, one hand on the bed for support. Standing, teetering, sitting back down.

"Dizzy?" Knowles asked. "Try it again. Take a deep breath."

Raider stood and walked the length of the bed, keeping one hand on it. When he reached the end he abandoned the support and shuffled about the room.

"Excellent!" exclaimed Knowles.

"Good going, Rade," said Doc encouragingly. "Now, get dressed, we've got work to do." Raider frowned and glanced at Knowles, his eyes inviting disagreement. He did not get it; the doctor nodded.

"Take a walk down to the end of the hall without touching the walls. Come back and tell us how you feel. Your legs'll feel watery, but that's to be expected. If you don't have any other problems—I'm talking about breathing—you can be discharged. This isn't a rest home. We need your bed. Okay, step out smartly."

Off he shuffled, out the door, down the corridor, weaving slightly, but maintaining an upright position without the assistance of either wall.

"He's the toughest piece of meat I've ever seen," said Knowles admiringly. "Bar none. I compared him to a brontosaurus. It fits. He's one of a kind. Nothing'll ever kill him; he'll live to a hundred and fifty, then become extinct."

The day after Ash Wednesday, which fell on the 23rd of February, nine of the accused murderers of David Hennessey—Bastion Incardona, Charles Matranga, Antonio Bagnetto, Antonio Marchesi, Joseph Madreca, Manuel Politz, Pietro Monasterio, Joseph Provenzano, and Enzo Carlone—were brought from the Old Parish Prison, at Conti and Orleans streets, to trial in Criminal Court in the Old New Orleans Courthouse before Judge Baker. A crowd estimated by the press at betwen ten and twelve thousand surrounded the building.

Raider, Doc, and Frank Montaigne met District Attorney, now Prosecutor Luzenberg outside the courtroom. They convened in the cloak room. Luzenberg's face was gray with concern. Doc half imagined that *he* was the one going on trial. Indeed it was all over. He'd been found guilty; he would hang.

"What . . ." began Montaigne.

Luzenberg waved him silent. "About twenty minutes ago,

just as I was leaving the office, I got some marvelous news. They've got the names of every juror, everyone subpoenaed for panel duty, sixty-three men."

"Didn't you expect that?" Doc asked.

"This isn't my first case, Weatherbee," he said acidly. "I know what we're up against. Do you? It's worse. Three talesmen have disappeared. Whether they just packed up and lit out after being threatened or were murdered and dumped in the bay, we don't know. Not yet. We're going into this thing with the Angel of Death hanging over us. If this keeps up, the whole pool'll evaporate. We won't find twelve men in the whole parish willing to serve. Would any of you, if you were threatened with murder and bombing?"

"District Attorney Luzenberg," called a voice outside.

"You're being paged," said Doc, opening the door. "Look, don't throw in the towel."

Luzenberg bristled. "Who the hell is throwing in the towel?"

"I mean . . ."

"I'm not overly interested in what you mean, mister!"

"Take it easy," said Raider. "How's this Judge Baker?"

"He's tamper-proof, if that's what you mean, and he keeps a firm hand on the reins. No shenanigans and no circuses in his court." Luzenberg sighed heavily. "Sixty-three talesmen won't be nearly enough. We're going to have to examine half the male population of New Orleans."

Unfortunately for the men of good faith concerned, the situation was to prove even more disheartening than the district attorney envisioned it as being. Among the spectators—more than two hundred of whom were permitted to attend the preliminary proceedings—were dozens of Mafia enforcers. When a talesman got up to be questioned by the court, the mobsters drew their fingers across their throats or held up thick wads of bills. Whenever either action occurred, Judge Baker would halt the proceedings, rap his gavel loudly, and order the offenders ejected. But as the day wore on it appeared that at least half of the spectators were representatives of the mob, and that every time one was ejected, another took his place.

It took four full days and more than eleven hundred talesmen were examined before a jury was finally selected. Witnesses who refused to be intimidated were placed under heavy guard by Luzenberg. One by one, these brave and honorable men were called uoon to step down from the witness stand, cross to the defense table, and, at Judge Baker's direction, touch the shoulder of and identify the nine defendants. One witness, a Negro, identified one of the defendants as the man who had fired the two shots that had killed Hennessey, insisting that he wore a piece of oilcloth over his shoulders. The oilcloth had been found by the police in the home of the accused during the citywide roundup. It was to become an important addition to the state's exhibits.

On the fifth day of the trial George Provenzano was called to testify. His written statement, earlier placed in evidence by Luzenberg, was continuously referred to as he was questioned. Raider brought to Doc's attention the fact that, throughout the questioning, George never looked at his brother Joe, and Joe never looked at him.

The five lawyers for the defense were among the most successful, capable, brilliant legal minds available. According to the *Times-Democrat,* their combined fee for defending the accused was estimated at well over one million dollars. Leading the defense team were Thomas J. Semmes, who claimed the distinction of never having lost a murder case in no fewer than thirty-four courtroom appearances, and Lionel Adams, a former district attorney. But the most valuable man engaged by the defense was Dominick C. O'Malley, a private detective. Lionel Adams was a partner in O'Malley's detective agency, providing a combination completely without precedent in the civilized world, according to the newspapers: partnership between a detective and a prominent criminal lawyer.

Wrote John C. Wickliffe, an editor on the New Orleans *Delta,* in a free-lance article appearing in *Frank Leslie's Illustrated Newspaper:*

"Convinced as the people were of the guilt of the accused, they were staggered by the strength of the case made out by the state. Eyewitnesses to the killing came forward and identified many of the men on trial. Circumstantial evidence of the most conclusive sort was piled on top of this. The momentum of the prosecution is daily increasing and bids fair to steamroller the Mafia into well-deserved oblivion. In the midst of the trial, Politz, one of the defendants, broke down and confessed that he was present at the meeting of the society when the death of Hennessey was decreed, and when the detail of murderers was made. He gave a partial list of the members, and gave their signs and signals. He confessed that Madreca, one of the defendants, had furnished the "Mafia gun' that was used, and had ordered him (Politz) to carry it to the house from which the assassins sallied when they killed Hennessey. This, of course, is only an outline of the confession."

On the seventh day of the trial, after a conference in Judge Baker's chambers with District Attorney Luzenberg and members of his staff and the lawyers for the defense present, the judge directed the acquittal of Charles Matranga on the grounds that the state had failed to offer sufficient evidence to link him with the murder. The state also agreed to abandon the prosecution of Bastion Incardona. Two doctors testified that Incardona's chronic heart condition and his advanced age (he was seventy-nine, and sat at the defense table in a wheelchair), combined with the stress of the proceedings, posed a grave risk to his "health and well-being."

When Judge Baker announced that the state had agreed to discontinue prosecution of Incardona, it was all Doc could do to keep from jumping up and protesting.

"The bastard," he fumed at Raider. "He didn't need any damned wheelchair at the Supreme Council meeting. He was as chipper as a nineteen-year-old!"

"Don't swear, Doc," whispered Raider. "Foul language purely offends me, you know that."

Frank Montaigne leaned into the conversation. "I don't give two hoots in a hollow about old Bastion, it's Guiseppe Esposito and Tony Matranga I'd like to get mah hooks into. They're the fust two should be climbing the gallows steps, and we can't even find 'em."

"You will," said Doc cheerfully.

Raider snorted derisively. "I'll bet you four dollars 'gainst a dead dog they're halfway back to Italy. With 'bout six million in gold in their damn satchels. You think they care 'bout this bunch? Hell, you know what they say 'bout honor 'mong thieves. Same holds for killers, you bet."

The case went to the jury the following day. Commented John C. Wickliffe in the New Orleans *Delta:*

"District Attorney Luzenberg and his staff, Lieutenant Frank Montaigne, and every policeman and detective in this city may be justifiably proud of their yeoman efforts in behalf of justice and decency. The state's case is ironclad; the accused are as guilty as Judas Iscariot. May his fate be their fate. May each and every one hang from the highest tree in Orleans Parish. Justice has triumphed! God's in his heaven! All's right with the world!"

The jury arrived at a verdict.

The verdict: not guilty.

CHAPTER EIGHTEEN

Absolute astonishment greeted announcement of the verdict.
Stunned disbelief settled silence over the packed courtroom.
Momentarily. Then it exploded, became a bedlam. The clamor
and shouting in the room and the halls outside was deafening,
threatening to shatter light fixtures and windows. Up went the
battle cry, "Hang the Dagos!" Two hundred policemen, arms
locked, encircled the building, while inside half that number
of bailiffs, clerks, and spectators able to bridle their outrage
struggled to control the mob and clear the building. At seven
o'clock in the evening, with the courtroom emptied of everyone
save the principals involved in the proceedings, Judge Baker
granted District Attorney Luzenberg's request that the defendants be returned to their cells in the Old Parish Prison to join
the other Mafia prisoners in order to give his office time to
investigate the verdict.

By nightfall lynch law controlled New Orleans. Pitched
battles erupted in the streets, the intermittent sound of gunfire
rang from City Park to Chartres Street. By ten o'clock every

cell in every station house in the city was crammed with citizens charged with everything from malicious mischief to murder. Torchlight parades wound through every district, outraged citizens carrying placards and posters denouncing the verdict, demanding a reversal, castigating the jurors, and threatening to hang all twelve. Judge Baker was lynched in effigy in four different locations. It speedily became apparent that the police, having filled all available cell space, were helpless to control the surging masses of people. Mayor Shakespeare appointed Attorney W. S. Parkerson, leader of the Citizens Committee of Fifty as "head of the movement to correct justice."

The sun rose over Lake Borgne the next morning, spreading its warmth over the seething city and revealing hundreds of posters urging "all good citizens to join in the fight to remedy the failure of justice in the Hennessey case."

District Attorney Luzenberg announced to the newspapers that the prosecution had in its possession irrefutable proof that the jury had been tampered with. J. M. Seligman, the foreman, a partner with his brother in a jewelry business; Walker Livandais, a clerk with the Southern-Pacific Railroad; and five other jurors had come forward and signed statements admitting that they had accepted bribes. As the day wore on and the disruption and sporadic violence intensified, it became obvious that Dominick C. O'Malley and his henchmen had systematically destroyed the state's "ironclad case" by the simple and effective expedient of distributing a fortune in Mafia money.

Meanwhile, the Italian colony was celebrating the verdict with unrestrainable joy. Stands in the French Market, owned by Sicilians, audaciously displayed bunting and streamers in the green, white, and red of the Italian flag. The flag of Italy was everywhere in evidence; overnight New Orleans had become Palermo on the Delta. Black handprints with the word *Vittoria* scrawled under them appeared on walls and windows, sidewalks, posters, and even the front doors of Judge Baker's, Prosecutor Luzenberg's, and Mayor Shakespeare's homes. In Old Parish Prison the acquitted defendants, although still under indictment for conspiracy, toasted each other and their lawyers with wine sent in by families, friends, and admirers. Madams and prostitutes by the score showered food and gifts on the eleven ringleaders. The word about the city, uttered in a heavy

Sicilian accent, as one newspaper noted, was that the Mafia was back on top to stay. Having beaten the best the state had to offer, it would resume running the town to suit itself. The *Times-Democrat* devoted a full page to a cartoon depicting a swarthy, menacing-looking, dagger-wielding Mafioso with a portion of the map of the city sticking out of his jacket pocket.

Many of the state's witnesses left town. George Provenzano refused to. Other witnesses barred their homes and stockpiled arms and ammunition. Down at the wharf a gang of Sicilians tore down an American flag, trampled it in the mud, spat upon it, urinated on it, and rehoisted it upside down under the Italian flag.

While the victors celebrated and the vanquished fumed in frustration and decried the blindness of justice and what the *Times-Picayune* termed her untimely demise at the hands of the "Black Hand's Blue Ribbon Jury," Attorney Parkerson's newly formed citizens' committee held a closed-door meeting in a Carondelet Street club. Strategy for reprisal was formulated and the wording of a public announcement agreed upon. A notice appeared in the morning papers:

MASS MEETING!

> All good citizens are invited to attend a
> mass meeting today at 10 o'clock a.m.,
> at Clay Statue, to take steps to remedy
> the failure of justice in the HENNESSEY
> CASE. Come prepared for

ACTION!

Sixty-one of New Orleans' most prominent citizens signed the notice. Three hours before the appointed time for the mass meeting, the Clay Statue was surrounded by a crowd so large it filled Canal Street and extended halfway up both Royal Street and St. Charles Avenue. Estimated at close to ten thousand by newspaper reporters, the crowd was made up of young and old, black and white, with the overwhelming majority representing the best element in the city.

Just before ten o'clock, the signers of the notice, sixty-one strong led by Attorney Parkerson, came marching three abreast down Canal Street. When they reached the statue, the crowd quickly swarmed around Parkerson. He was in his late sixties, tall, with a craggy, Lincolnesque face, a commanding appearance, and the mellifluous voice of an accomplished soliloquist capable of riveting jurors in the box and manipulating their emotions as dexterously and easily as a puppeteer manipulates his papier-mâcheé performers. Calling for attention, he solemnly requested the crowd to form a line. At the head of his sixty co-signers of the public announcement, followed by the crowd, he circled the monument three times. Then he assumed the pedestal while his sixty associates took up positions against the railing enclosing the statue.

Calling for silence, Parkerson began: "People of New Orleans. Once before I stood before you for public duty. I now appear before you again actuated by no desire for fame or prominence. Affairs have reached such a crisis that men living in an organized and civilized community, finding their laws fruitless and ineffective, are forced to protect themselves. When courts fail, the people must act. What protection or assurance of protection is there left us when the very head of our Police Department, our Chief of Police, is assassinated in our very midst by the Mafia Society and his assassins are again turned loose on the community? Will every man here follow me and see the murder of Hennessey avenged?"

A deafening roar rose from the crowd. Once more he silenced his listeners.

"Are there men enough here to set aside the verdict of that infamous jury, every one of whom is a perjurer and a scoundrel?"

Again, the roar.

"There is another viper in our midst, and that is Dominick C. O'Malley. This community must get rid of the man who has had the audacity to enter a libel suit against one of our daily papers that boldly came out and denounced him to the public in his true colors. I now, right here, publicly, openly, and fearlessly denounce him as a suborner and procurer of witnesses and a briber of juries. Men and citizens of New Orleans, follow me! I will be your leader."

The roar erupting from the multitude was like the crashing of thunder. Mr. William Denegre, a prominent businessman, took Parkerson's place on the pedestal, but his opening words were drowned by the cries of the crowd. Quiet was finally restored, and Denegre spoke briefly, echoing Parkerson's challenge. Editor John C. Wickliffe followed in the same denunciatory manner, saying among other things that self-preservation is the first law of nature, and that the time had come for the citizens of New Orleans to protect themselves against "the eleven-headed poisonous serpent temporarily reposing in Old Parish Prison, and soon to be let loose once more upon our helpless community.

"Let us therefore act, fellow citizens. Fall in under the leadership of W. S. Parkerson. James D. Houston will be your first lieutenant. And I, J. C. Wickliffe, will be your second lieutenant."

The inflammatory rhetoric had its desired effect, transforming the crowd into a mob. Detached from it, standing on either side of a street lamp, Raider and Doc exchanged worried glances.

"I didn't think this mess could get any worse," remarked Raider, "but it's fixing to. Parkerson and those other two must be loco!"

"They've had all they can take, Rade." Doc shook his head. "A half hour from now, that prison is going to be knee-deep in blood."

Wickliffe had stepped down from the pedestal; it was the signal for the mob to turn and begin streaming in the direction of the prison. The committee members led by Parkerson, Houston, and Wickliffe formed ranks and marched to a gun store at the corner of Royal and Bienville. There they armed themselves with pistols, rifles, and shotguns. Raider and Doc followed them toward the prison, continuing to keep their distance.

Not a policeman was in sight.

The march on the prison had an electric effect on the city. The streets surrounding the sprawling brick complex were suddenly alive with people running from all directions, joining the main body moving sullenly down Rampart Street. Doors and windows flew open, and men, women, and children crowded on the galleries shouting encouragement and tossing down tools and anything else that could be used as weapons.

By the time the main crowd from Canal Street reached the prison nearly two thousand people had already collected before the front doors. Lieutenant Montaigne, anticipating trouble, had left the station long before the speeches began at the Clay Statue, going directly to the prison. Sheriff Villere, having heard rumors that an attempt would be made to storm the prison and seize the eleven assassins, armed fifteen deputies and started on a hunt for Mayor Shakespeare. The Italian counsul and Attorney General Rogers joined in the quest, but upon reaching City Hall, they were told that His Honor was not expected until noon. Nor was he to be found at his club or any other of his regular haunts. Captain Lemuel Davis, a war hero and for seven years warden of the prison, discussed the situation and its ominous potential with Montaigne in the warden's office. They decided that all inmates other than the Italian suspects were to be locked in their cells while the Italians would be given the run of the prison and told to hide wherever they could. Warden Davis then went to the main entrance with six deputies to confront the mob.

The committee led by Parkerson and his two lieutenants arrived, pushing through to the front of the mob, all of whom were now armed with firearms, daggers, and sabers, as well as brickbats, baseball bats, and ax handles. The warden ordered the main doors bolted and cross-timbered. Parkerson's demand to be admitted was refused, whereupon a group of men armed with axes was dispatched around the corner into Marais Street with orders to break down the side entrance, a heavy wooden door. Attacking it with axes proved ineffectual. A lamp post was pulled down and used as a battering ram. It easily broke down the door. Inside, meanwhile, the prisoners were terror-stricken, cowering in their cells and wherever else they could find to hide, listening to the shouting outside.

Parkerson led his men inside. Each of them carried a list of the eleven prisoners believed guilty of Hennessey's murder. Each had explicit instructions not to harm any of the other Italians, or other prisoners.

The mob followed Parkerson and his men inside, seizing the few prison guards and deputies, disarming them and pushing them outside. By now the prison was surrounded on all sides by the jeering, cursing, screaming mob. The turnkey was found, overpowered, and his key taken from him. Outside, meanwhile, a patrol wagon drove up with a detachment of police from the Central Station, but they were quickly driven away under a barrage of rocks. Parkerson and his men, now in possession of the keys to every cell in the prison, opened the first cell they came to. A group of trembling prisoners huddled in a corner. They were not Sicilians, the door was relocked, and they were left unharmed. Proceeding on their way, the committee members rounded a corner, coming up on the condemned row. Peering through the bars of the second cell was a terror-stricken face which someone in the group mistook for Rocco Gerace. Six shots were fired at him at close range, and he fell, but miraculously, not a single bullet struck him, and it was quickly determined that he was not one of the assassins.

"Go to the womens' department!" he called.

Off ran Parkerson and the others. The door to the womens' department was locked. The proper key was found on the turn-key's ring, and in rushed the vigilantes. The gallery was deserted, but an old woman prisoner sputtered that the men they were looking for were upstairs. Eight men led by Wickliffe raced up the stairs. As they reached the landing, the assassins heard them coming and fled to the other end. When the pursued and their pursuers reached the stone courtyard, the assassins darted toward the Orleans Street side of the gallery, crowding against the wall and screaming for mercy.

The response was a hail of bullets. Rocco Gerace was struck seven times in the back of the head, shattering his skull into fragments, his body pitching forward and lying immobile on the stone pavement. Joseph Madreca fell to his knees, with his face in his hands, and died with at least twenty shots in his upper body and head. Joe Provenzano and James Caruso fell together under the fire of half a dozen guns, blood spurting from their wounds, Caruso's left eye shot from its socket, hanging grotesquely from one muscle.

In less than sixty seconds seven of the assassins were executed, and their blood-soaked corpses left where they fell. Two others, crouching in a large box under a stairway where Warden Davis's pet bullterrier slept, were discovered, and bludgeoned to death with ball bats. Both were decapitated and their heads smashed into flattened masses of unrecognizable gore.

Manuel Politz was dragged from a closet and shot in the chest but only wounded. His clothes were then ripped from his body, he was castrated with a saber and carried away to the corner of Tremé and St. Ann streets. There a rope was secured and he was hanged, still alive, from a lamp post. So many shots were fired into his body, the added weight eventually snapped the rope, tumbling his corpse to the pavement.

Politz was the next to the last of the eleven to be executed. It fell to John Wickliffe to seal the coffin. Inspecting the pile of corpses in the upstairs gallery, he discovered Antonio Bagnetto shamming death. Summoning four men, Wickliffe had Bagnetto dragged from the gallery. To the accompaniment of the sort of enthusiastic cheering and applause one might more likely associate with a sporting event, Bagnetto was hanged from a tree in front of the prison on Orleans Street, his swaying body pelted with stones and rotten fruit.

Less than an hour after the vigilantes broke into the prison, Parkerson climbed onto a windowsill, called for attention, and announced to the mob that "justice" had been done. The eleven suspects had been found and "executed."

"Executed," murmured Doc, his tone tinged with sarcasm. "Justice."

He and Raider watched from across the street as, moments later, Parkerson, beaming, pumping his upraised fist triumphantly, marched his party out the front door and into the embrace of a swarm of well-wishers. Raising him onto the shoulders of the two biggest men available, the hero of the hour was carried through Rampart and Canal streets at the head of shouting, ecstatic thousands.

The procession made its way back to the Clay Statue, where Parkerson called upon the crowd to disperse. Many left, but hundreds lingered. Wickliffe made his second speech of the day. Said he: "I ask you all, as an endorsement of what has been done, and in pursuance of the promise which we impliedly gave the people, to return quietly to your homes. The lesson we have given will have its effect. If it does not, we will repeat it."

There would be no need to "repeat it." The serpent's neck had been broken. Newspapers denounced the lynchings and the wholesale slaughter of the seven in the upstairs gallery, demanding investigations by the authorities, but the man on the street wholeheartedly approved of the actions of the mob.

Declared Mayor Shakespeare: "I do consider that the act was, however deplorable, a necessity and justifiable. The Italians had taken the law into their own hands, and we had to do the same."

CHAPTER NINETEEN

The Mafia was dead in New Orleans, but Esposito and Tony Matranga remained at large, and while they did Frank Montaigne kept the case file open and the investigation as to their whereabouts full scale. In the days that followed, sixty-three Sicilians were scheduled to be deported, and nearly three times that number were tried and sentenced to prison terms on charges varying from extortion and accessory to murder to grand larceny, bribery, vice, political corruption, and virtually every other felony and misdemeanor in the catalog of crime. Dominick C. O'Malley was discovered in his office shot through the head; the police had no clue as to his killer. The continuing investigation established that roughly two-thirds of the politicians, judges, and other public servants in the city were on the Mafia payroll. They were speedily rounded up and charged.

The *Picayune* assembled additional evidence of jury foreman Jacob Seligman's involvement with the mob and presented it to District Attorney Luzenberg. The Stock Exchange held an extraordinary meeting and expelled Seligman. His brother dissolved their partnership in their jewelry business. Among other charges leveled at Seligman was the accusation that prior to the trial he had made wagers involving large sums that the jury would bring in a verdict of not guilty.

George Provenzano went back to work on the wharf. He assembled his employees and announced that their original pay scale would be reinstated and that henceforth no man with a criminal record would hold a job in any capacity with Provenzano Banana Importing.

Raider and Doc returned from visiting George to find visitors of their own waiting in the hotel lobby. The younger, shapelier, and prettier of the two was furious at Doc.

"Y'all leave a note that y'all are coming back at ten o'clock next day and you never show up! Y'all call that any way to treat a lady, *Mr*. Hastings-Weatherbee!"

Raider glanced about the lobby; all eyes previously concentrating on newspapers were suddenly concentrating on them.

"Billy, will you for chrissakes keep it down? Emma, she's downright embarrassing."

"Y'all shut your face, John!" She caught herself. "Are you all right? Y'all fit again? You look like death warmed up in a pan."

"Thanks."

"Billy," began Doc, "you know what happened that next morning. We were at the Old Parish Prison watching the show. I apologize for not getting back to you."

She grabbed Raider's arm possessively. "He coulda been lying in that old hospital dead as Dulcie Mae for all Ah'd know 'bout it. Some fine friend you are!" She paused and shifted her eyes between Doc and Emma Pickett. "Oh, pardon mah bad manners, you two don't know each othah. This heah's Miz Emma Pickett, mah formah and soon-to-be-again employah, er, landlady. This is Mr. Weatherbee, Em."

"How do you do," gushed Emma, posing her considerable bulk as daintily as her dimensions allowed and switching on her most disarming smile.

"We'all got news foh you two," said Billy, lowering her voice. "Let's go somewheres where we can jaw."

"We could jaw here," rasped Raider, "if you weren't so loud in the mouth."

Doc swept a hand toward the street door. "It's a lovely day.

Let's promenade." He chivalrously offered his arm to Emma. She tittered and laid hold. Raider stifled a grin.

Outside the sun blazed furiously. The scent of magnolias hung in the air.

"Guess what!" burst out Billy. "We know wheah you know who is. Emma does, don'tcha, Em? Tell 'em, Em. The whole entiah city's looking foh Mr. E., and we know wheah he's hiding, him and that fat butter tub, Matranga. Tell 'em, Em. Theah wheah nobody'd dream they'd be, in Mr. E.'s little old house ovah on Chartres. Tell 'em, Em. Place is fulla secret rooms and such. Theah safer than two coons in a hollow log, tell 'em, Em."

"Tell us, Em," muttered Raider.

She sighed, "What's to tell?"

"Are you positive they're there?" Doc asked. "Who says so?"

"Word's all over the street," said Emma.

Raider snorted. "Rumor, you mean."

"He's the grateful one," said Billy to Emma. "Mr. Doubtin' Thomas. Ever' time ah bring him infohmation he kicks a hole smack through it."

"Frank Montaigne should know about this, Rade. Let's get over to the station." He loosened Emma's hold on his arm. Raider did the same with Billy's, bringing a pained expression to her pretty face.

"Let us come," she said.

Doc shook his head. "It's police business, Billy. We can't."

She tugged at Raider's sleeve. "Then when am Ah gonna see you again, John?"

"Ahhh, tonight. The Bird Cage. Nine o'clock."

"Nine o'clock's working hours, dear heart," said Emma sweetly. "Why don't you two come around to the house? You know the address, Mr. Wilson."

"How could I ever forget."

Lieutenant Montaigne, Raider, Doc, and four uniforms marched across General Jackson's shadow in the center of Jackson Square in the direction of Chartres Street and Esposito's house. Doc's feelings became decidedly mixed as they drew within sight of its familiar, ivy-framed front door. They were less than fifty yards away, and Raider's hand was lifting from his side and coming to rest on the grip of his Peacemaker, when a tremendous explosion occurred. The roof rose, the walls distended, the front door blew forth in a cloud of black smoke, tongues of flame burst from the windows upstairs and down, and the entire building collapsed, fragments of the roof descending, landing in the burning rubble. Bricks flew in every direction. The group approaching had broken ranks and thrown themselves to the ground. A brick landed three feet from Raider's head, bounced lightly, and came to rest.

"Jesus Christ!" exclaimed one of the policemen, rising slowly to his hands and knees and gaping in disbelief. The house was completely destroyed, the explosion so powerful the end walls were propelled against the houses on either side, caving in their walls. People came running from all directions. The wail of a fire siren came drifting on the breeze from the square behind them.

Two bodies were found in the rubble, both charred beyond recognition.

"Esposito and Matranga," asserted Montaigne. "Fiah chief says they were both found in an undahground anteroom of some soht. He seems to think the two of 'em had set up tempohrary housekeeping theah. All the neighbohs the boys talked to claim the house was closed up tight. Had been since befoh the raid on the prison, even befoh the trial. Blinds drawn, no lights at night, nobody seen coming or going."

"Isn't the coroner going to examine the bodies?" asked Doc.

The lieutenant nodded. He was busy cleaning out the drawers of his desk as he talked, preparing to move into Hennessey's office.

"Mattah o' procedure. You saw 'em. They don't look human; look moh like two-legged fence posts. Grisly. Helluva way to go."

Raider, sucking on a toothpick, pulled it from his mouth and ran the tip of his tongue across his upper teeth.

"One sure thing. If the coroner can't identify them, nobody else is gonna. You think maybe that's what old Giuseppe and his pal are counting on? I mean, think 'bout it, Doc, why would they go and blow themselves up?"

"I wish I could say 'good question.' Really, Rade, obviously somebody else did the honors."

Raider shrugged. "Either that or they went to a lotta trouble to make it look like somebody else did."

"Why don't we wait and see what the cohoneh has to say," suggested Montaigne.

"He's not going to tell us anything we don't know. No sir, I can smell a setup from six miles upwind. And this is as slick as they come. I mean think about it. Esposito's the big chief, king o' the hill. When the balloon goes up he decides he'll disappear with 'bout six or seven million bucks. Him and his best buddy. Gone, vanished. You be Matranga, Doc, I'll be Giuseppe. Here we are with satchels fulla money and the whole world's collapsing. Only we can't be a hundred percent sure it will, not with all the cash we're spreading round to the jury and witnesses and practically everybody connected with the trial except the D.A. and the judge. Then in comes the verdict, not guilty. So what do you figure? You're off the hook, right? So you hang around. Why leave when you don't have to? Only then comes the massacre."

"Making for a slight change in plans," said Doc, nodding.

"Right. Can't stick round now. Gotta go. Where to?"

"I know where Ah'd go," said Montaigne. "Home."

Doc nodded. "Sicily." His expression of agreement darkened. "Maybe not. He's wanted in Sicily for the murder of that English minister, remember? How can he go back?"

"Oh, for chrissakes, Doc, that was a long time ago. It's all blown over. Besides, he's a rich man, he can buy back his reputation as a fine, upstanding pillar o' the community."

"He can indeed," said Montaigne. "That's the way of the world."

"So he and Tony decide to get out," continued Raider. "Only it makes sense to cover their tracks, right? So what do they do? They get a couple o' their admirers to come over for tea, get 'em down into that room on some . . . what's the word, Doc?"

"Pretext."

"Lock 'em in, light the fuse, and hightail it outta there."

A light tapping at the door glass drew their eyes. George Provenzano stood beaming, a newspaper folded under one arm. Montaigne welcomed him effusively.

"Ah thought you were back in hahness?"

"I am. But I was out on the wharf talking with some of the

boys, you know, and I heard something interesting, something you might appreciate knowing, *capish?*" He closed the door and lowered his voice. "You hear about Esposito and Tony Matranga?"

Raider threw up his hands. "I swear, news travels faster'n damn greased lightning in this town. Who told you?"

"You know about their getting out. Tonight."

Raider stared. "That's not what I'm talking—"

Montaigne cut in. "George, back up a little. Did you know Esposito's house blew up?"

He had not heard about it. Montaigne explained. To nobody's surprise, George immediately voiced his own suspicion that the explosion was planned for the obvious reason. He unfolded his paper, spreading it on the desk and leafing to the next to the last page: "Shipping Arrivals and Departures." He ran a finger down the list of ships.

"See this? The *Star of Messina.* Messina, mean anything to you?"

"Sicily," said Doc.

"They're getting out on this ship." George tapped the paper. "I'll bet my life on it. It's the only one on the list going back to the old country. It says it's sailing at seven tonight. It's carrying a cargo of cotton and thirteen passengers. Eleven human beings and two two-legged *serpenti.*"

A plan of action was quickly devised. It didn't seem likely that either man would be traveling as a passenger. They would probably be posing as members of the crew. According to George, the crew would have to report for duty back on board at least two hours before sailing time. It was decided that Raider and Doc would board the ship at five o'clock. Montaigne, meanwhile, would go to the Immigration Office and iron out the technicalities involved. Neither Tony Matranga nor Giuseppe Esposito had become naturalized American citizens; arresting and removing Italian nationals from an Italian vessel, even though it was berthed in an American port, could conceivably raise problems, and Montaigne wanted to be sure he was on firm legal ground when he requested—if necessary, demanded—permission of the *Messina*'s captain to remove the two Mafiosi.

"Aftah all, those two are going to be carrying enough money to bribe everybody on boahd."

"If you run into a legal snag, we could get the port master to delay the sailing," suggested Doc.

"I don't know," said Montaigne, "but the boys down to Immigration do. It could get mighty sticky. I think I ought to alert the D.A.'s office, too."

Doc nodded agreement with this. Raider did not.

"This broth is beginning to take on too many cooks. Why you even bothering with Immigration? Why not just get warrants from Judge Baker or some other gavel rapper, go on board, roust 'em out, and lock 'em up?"

"We already got outstanding warrants on both," said Montaigne.

"Rade, it's just not that simple. It's true, we *think* the two bodies found in the house aren't Matranga and Esposito . . ."

"Cut the horseshit, you know goddamn well they aren't!"

"That's the trouble, we don't."

"He's right," said Montaigne. "Look, I'll see to all the technical doings. You two just get down to the docks by five at the latest, show youah I.D.s—I'll give you a couple aids or officahs, if you like—you just find those two. Tuhn the ship upside down if you have to, but find 'em."

The *Star of Messina* was a rust-splotched, overage vagrant, sorely in need of scraping and painting. Twin gray stacks with black collars rose from her well deck. Her holds were loaded, her passengers and crew on board, and she was prepared to sail. The harbor offered certain natural advantages. No tug service was needed, for docking at least, and situated at the mouth of the river, it was tideless, enabling ships to come and go at any hour they pleased.

The skies overhead were littered with seabirds, the docks below overrun with rats. The ships berthed on either side of the *Star* ran the gamut from a sleek-looking British merchantman to a listing, barely serviceable Mexican cattle boat, reeking with the stink of manure, and four wretched-looking luggers, stinking of rotten fish and oysters.

Captain Sebastian greeted Raider and Doc in his cabin, to which they were escorted by a burly-looking and seemingly mute third officer. They showed their I.D.s and explained their visit. The captain, a stumpy little man with meticulously pomaded hair plastered across his pate and a flowing handlebar mustache under his huge nose, seemed shocked at their disclosure. He studied the somewhat blurred photograph of Esposito and shook his head.

"He is not a passenger. You have a picture of the other one?"

Doc took his turn at shaking his head. "When we find one," he assured him, "we'll find the other."

Sebastian showed the picture to his third mate. He, too, shook his head. As yet he had not uttered a single word.

"If they're not passengers, they could be with the crew," suggested Raider. "If they're not crew, they got to be stowing away."

Sebastian grinned, showing crooked, tobacco-stained teeth. "No one stows away on my ship, gentlemen. That, I can assure you. If you wish, I will instruct the first mate to assemble the men on deck. You can question them. You can see for yourselves."

He started to speak to the third mate in Italian. Raider held up his hand, interrupting.

"No call to go through all that rigmarole," he said.

Doc stared at him. "What are you saying? How else are we supposed—"

"Doc, use your head." He paused, looking toward the captain, then at the third mate. "Would you mind excusing us just a shake?"

He stepped outside on deck, pulling Doc with him.

"Rade . . ."

"Just shut up and listen, okay? No matter what old plaster hair and his boy in there say, we *know* they're on board. They maybe don't, but we do. They got to be. They wouldn't be coming aboard two minutes afore she sails. You can waste time lining up everybody on board—passengers, officers, crew, even the kid that wallops the pots in the gallery—"

"Galley."

"Whatever. Nobody's gonna know beans. Now, this is how I figure it. Matranga and Espo got money to burn, right? So they make a deal with somebody to sneak 'em on board and hide 'em. Lock 'em up someplace, behind the damn engine or somewheres where nobody goes. Whoever's helping 'em will bring 'em their food, wait on 'em hand and foot, but most important of all, keep 'em under wraps until this tub gets where it's going. Is that right or is that right?"

"It's an interesting hypothesis. There's a modicum of logic—"

"Oh, cut the goatshit, will you? I'm dead center the bull's-eye and you know it? The big question is, who would they make the deal with?"

"That could be almost anyone . . . except perhaps the passengers."

"Not the captain."

"Probably not. No matter how big a bribe they offered, he'd be risking his master's ticket."

"Who's boss over the crew, that third-mate guy?"

"The first mate."

"Ahhh, he's the one I want to talk to."

"He'd be the logical one for them to approach, but do you think you can get him to admit he smuggled them aboard? Why would he open up to you, a stranger, a Pinkerton no less? Talk about wasting time!"

"I just want to chin with the man, just him and me. What's better—to waste a whole hour, maybe more, lining everybody up and showing 'em Espo's picture, asking questions, everybody shaking their heads, turning this tub upside down searching, like Montaigne said to? That, or this? Think about it, Doc, we could search for six weeks. A ship this size they could hide anyplace. They could move round while we're looking, keeping one step ahead. Whoever's in cahoots with 'em would help 'em."

"We could blow the whistle and bring fifty uniforms on board, start at the bow in the crew's quarters and sweep the ship full length."

"That's the hard way. Can't you for chrissakes listen to reason once in your life?"

"You mean do it your way."

"Give me twenty damn minutes."

Captain Sebastian and the third mate appeared in the doorway.

"It is almost five-thirty, gentlemen. We sail at seven."

"Captain, with your permission we'd like to speak to your first mate," said Doc.

"Mr. Spallone? By all means. Bartolomeo . . ."

The third mate touched the peak of his cap in salute and walked off.

A brief difference of opinion ensued between the two Pinkertons before Doc agreed to let Raider speak to Spallone alone.

"I just don't want him thinking we're ganging up on him, Doc. I got me an idea that just might work."

"What are you going to do?"

They stood at the railing, their backs to the captain's cabin door. Overhead three seagulls carved the still air, shrieking antagonistically at one another, as if each was claiming the space as private territory and wanted the other two out of there. Down the line of ships a lugger sounded its plaintive whistle. The brilliant orange sun was lowering, preparing to immerse itself in Lac des Allemands in the west.

"Why do you want to know?" responded Raider impatiently. "Let me just try. If I mess up, you take it from there."

"No rough stuff, Rade, promise me. No threats, no hand on the heel of your gun."

"Sssh, here he comes with the big boy."

Doc started off, touching his hat brim to and exchanging smiles with a pretty young woman carrying a parasol and a Pekingese. The third and first mates approached Raider. The third mate went into Captain Sebastian's cabin, leaving First Mate Umberto Spallone with Raider.

"You wish to speak to me, *signor?*"

"You're the first mate . . ."

"*Si, si,* for going on six years now." He flung his arms out in the manner of an opera singer melodically embracing the world. "On this beautiful ship. Is it not beautiful? And most seaworthy. In my time we have crossed the Atlantic a hundred and three times."

"Yeah, yeah." Raider produced Esposito's picture. "Recognize this fella?"

Spallone studied the photograph, his brows furrowing, his lower lip pushing upward, crinkling his beardless chin. He shook his head.

"I have never seen him before in my life. I would know. That is a face one would remember."

"He's a very famous man. His name is Giuseppe Esposito. He's Mafia."

Spallone reacted startled. "A criminal?"

"The worst. The biggest in New Orleans. In the whole state, maybe even the country. He's going back to Sicily. My partner and I think he mighta sneaked on board this ship."

"A stowaway? Aboard the *Star of Messina*. Impossible! You have wrong information, Mr. . . . ."

"Raider."

"Mr. Raider, we have not had one single stowaway in all my years on this ship. The owners are very strict. There are rules and regulations every member of the crew must follow to the letter. They are printed in English, Italian, Portuguese, Greek—at least nine languages. Assisting a stowaway is a criminal offense, as you know. If any of my men were to attempt such a thing, he would be instantly discharged. No, the *Star of Messina* permits no stowaways."

He returned the picture to Raider.

"Well, that sure is good to hear. My partner and I were real worried. O' course, you'd know, wouldn't you? I mean in your job you have to know everything goes on with your crew."

"Everything. No secret is safe from Umberto Spallone. I have eyes in the back of my head. My men know that, they toe the line."

Raider chuckled good-naturedly. "You probably even know their wives' names, the names o' their little ones . . ."

"Of course. We are like a big family. Rarely does a hand quit the *Star*. And because that is so, we have no need to hire new hands. We are all like brothers."

"You a family man yourself?"

"*Si, si,* I have a wife and six children."

"Six? My, my, my."

"You too are married?"

"No, I'm sorry to say I'm not that fortunate. Just never got round to marrying."

Spallone clucked sympathetically, his handsome face sagging. "A pity. My family is the joy of my life. That is the only drawback to my career, the prolonged absences from home."

"I bet. Well, you're heading home now. You'll be seeing 'em soon. I envy you being married, having a family. I'm crazy 'bout kids myself."

"Ahhhh, you must allow me to show you mine."

He brought out a somewhat battered wallet. Holding it up, he displayed his family standing in a group, squinting into the sun.

"What a fine-looking family. Your wife is some beautiful lady!"

"Celestina. She is a singer, a voice like a nightingale." He beamed proudly.

Raider casually took the wallet from him to further study the picture. Spallone continued beaming. Raider's thumb and forefinger joined to probe the bill envelope. Very slowly he pulled forth the contents. Spallone's smile vanished; he snatched at the wallet.

"What are you doing! Give me that!"

Raider held it teasingly over the railing. Spallone blanched.

"Be careful, you will drop it!"

Raider pulled the wallet close. "You got yourself some pile here, mister. One, two . . . five five-hundred-dollar bills. That's bi-i-i-g money. You boys riding the scows make a good day's pay, don't you?"

"I, ah . . . I won it gambling."

He snatched back his wallet, stuffing it into his back pocket.

"Where 'bouts?"

"In New Orleans, where do you think?"

"What, shooting craps?"

"Faro."

"You trying to tell me you won twenty-five hundred bucks playing faro? You must be a goddamn riverboat pro!" He frowned. "Okay, let's quit dancing round the candle and get straight. There's no game in town, faro or otherwise, pays off in crisp new five-hundred-dollar bills. 'Sides, you're a family man. Family men don't gamble heavy. Most don't gamble at all. You want me to tell you where you got it? Or do you tell me?"

He leaned closer, hardening his tone. "Two men paid you to smuggle 'em on board. The one in the picture I showed you, and another."

"No, no, no, you are mistaken!"

Raider grabbed his arm. "Let's go see the captain."

"No, no, please! Merciful God!" He jerked free. He had paled and was suddenly extremely nervous. He licked his lips.

"We can keep this between us, can we not? Are we both not gentlemen of the world? Can we not come to an understanding? One hand washes the other..."

"Every day. Tell you what, I'm not greedy. You give me four, and you can keep one."

"That is unfair! It is outrageous!"

Raider took him by the arm again, walking him slowly up the deck. "I'm only funning you, Umberto. I don't want your money. All I want is those two. Where you got 'em hid?"

Spallone's shoulders sagged and he emptied his lungs with a loud whooshing sound. "There is only one."

"Which, Esposito or Matranga?"

"Neither. His name is Pietro Gambelli. He is a wealthy businessman. The police are looking for him for a crime he did not commit. He is entirely innocent. It is his twin brother—"

"Oh for chrissakes, cut the horseshit! Where you got him?"

"In my cabin."

"Where? Goddamn it, talk! Don't make me pull it outta you word by word!"

The first mate held up a brass key. "It is forward below." He nodded toward the companionway. "My name is on the door."

"Rade..."

Doc had come up behind them.

"Doc, hang onto this one. I got something I got to do."

"But—"

"Don't let him outta your sight. I'll be back in two shakes. It's jack-pot time, get set to bust out the champagne!"

CHAPTER TWENTY

Esposito stared, his dark eyes incredulous. "You!"

Raider shut the door behind him. "Me. Aren't you gonna ask me what I want?"

The surprise becoming fear slowly deserted the little man's face. "What everybody wants, eh?" He was in his shirt-sleeves, hanging up a neatly pressed white linen suit on the back of the closet door. He turned his attention back to the suit, dusting down the lapels with the edge of his hand, picking off a bit of lint. At the foot of the bed was a fancy, brass-cornered trunk, its barrel-stave top open, its contents partially unpacked. Esposito turned to it, thrusting his hand into it.

Raider's hand went for his gun. "Watch it!"

Esposito smirked. Shoving aside two shirts still buttoned in their cardboards, he brought out a tin box the size of a shoe box. Closing the trunk, he set it on top and opened it, revealing banded stacks of new bills.

"Oh, boy," murmured Raider dispiritedly.

"Looks good, eh, cowboy? Money never looks bad. How much you think is there?"

"Close it up, straighten your tie, pick up the box, and let's go."

Esposito pretended he didn't even hear him, his smile sticking in place. "About fifty t'ousand." He held out two of the four stacks, "Half for you. Before you go, you count it, eh? I wouldn't want to short you."

"Whatta day," murmured Raider. "Everybody wants to give me money."

"You no like money? Twenny-five t'ousand, that's more than you make four, five years, eh?"

"Put it back in the box. Answer me a question, where's your friend, Matranga?"

"He go someplace." He shrugged. "He no tell me."

"With his brother Charlie?"

A second shrug. A gleam crept into Raider's eyes. "They went away, or did they go visiting? Maybe a certain house on Chartres Street? Went for a little visit and got into a little accident?"

"I don't know what you talking about."

His expression said otherwise. A knock sounded behind Raider. The door opened. He stood to one side. Doc and Captain Sebastian stood staring, the captain utterly mystified. Spallone, behind him, was white-faced, looking to Raider as if he were contemplating jumping over the rail.

"Doc, meet Mr. Piertro Gambelli, otherwise known as Giuseppe Esposito. Giuseppe, this is my partner, Mr. Weatherbee. Look what he wants to give me, Doc."

"I do not understand any of this," began Captain Sebastian. "Who is this man?" he asked Spallone.

"Tell him, Umberto," said Raider. "Level with him, it could go easier for you."

Sebastian did not wait for explanation. He began castigating Umberto in Italian. They stood jabbering at each other, Sebastian pushing him up the deck. Raider beckoned Doc inside and closed the door.

"You're incredible, Rade, I've really got to hand it to you."

Raider grunted.

"This is getting expensive," growled Esposito. He picked up the money box and thrust it at Doc. "Take it, split it, okay? Take it and get out."

"We don't want your money," said Doc evenly, "but if you'd like to make a contribution..."

"Contribution?"

"To Captain Hennessey's widow. We're starting a fund."

"Yeah," said Raider, "here and now. Congratulations, you're the first contributor. You're a generous man, Giuseppe."

Esposito tossed his hand. "Sure, for Captain Hennessey's widow. Whatever you say."

Doc tucked the box under one arm. "Now, where's the rest?"

"That's it, all I got. Every penny."

"You're a goddamn liar!" Raider's hand went to his gun.

"Easy, Rade. Giuseppe, get your gear together, we're leaving."

His face fell. "You crazy! I just give you..."

Raider glared. "You give us nothing, you bastard. This here is for the Hennessey fund."

Another knock. Doc opened the door to a young, blond Scandinavian deckhand.

"Mr. Pinkertons? The captain says to tell you that the police have come on board."

"Montaigne," said Raider. "I'll stick here and collect the rest o' the loot. He's gonna look for it for me. It's here, it's gotta be. Keep Montaigne busy. Tell him not to bother looking for Matranga. Those two bodies in the house were him and his brother. Bet your life on it. Mr. Hair here puts a real high price on loyalty and friendship."

"No rough stuff, Rade. Give me your gun."

"You think I'm gonna shoot him? And miss out on the hanging and all the fun?"

Doc had his hand out. "I'm doing you a favor. I'm removing temptation."

"Okay, okay." He handed him his Peacemaker.

"And the knife."

"It's back at the hotel. What the hell is this? Whose side you on, anyways?"

Doc withdrew.

"Okay, Espo," said Raider. "Let's cut the bullshit in half and get down to cases. How much you got with you, five million, ten? You want to trot it out, or do I pull your beard outta your face for starters?"

• • •

Doc handed the box to Montaigne. "Fifty thousand in cash, give or take a little bribe money. Friend Esposito's contribution to the Hennessey fund, for David's widow and children."

"Are you serious?"

"He gave it to us of his own free will. For just that purpose."

Montaigne handed the box to a uniformed policeman. "Wheah's Raidah?"

"With our friend. They're in the first mate's cabin. He's collecting the rest of Esposito's retirement fund. He'll be bringing it and him up shortly."

Montaigne's face darkened. "I kinda got some bad news foh you, Doc. Weah not going to be taking him in."

"What are you talking about? We've got a list of charges against him that'd reach from here to Mandeville. Plus a double murder this morning."

Montaigne was shaking his head. "I got the word about an houh ago from Luzenberg's office. He got it from Attohney General Rogers, straight from Govehnoh Nicholls. Mayoh Shakespeah put a flea in the govehnoh's eah."

"Frank, what are you saying?"

"They want Esposito depohted. No arrest, no trial, no moh three-ring cihcuses is the way the mayoh put it. Today's *Times-Democrat* quotes the govehnoh as describing the massacre at the prison as a Cahnival of Death. The whole filthy business has left a bad taste in everybody's mouth." He shrugged. "I can't honestly say I blame them. They just don't want a repeat perfohmance, Doc."

Doc threw up his hands. "Marvelous!"

Montaigne produced the warrant for Esposito's arrest and also Tony Matranga's. Crumpling them, he tossed them over the railing. "I'm sorry, sorrier than you know, but ohdehs are ohdehs." He grinned. "Theah is some good news. I just got wohd befoh I left the office I been made captain."

"Captain Montaigne. Great, you deserve it. Congratulations."

"Thanks kindly." Montaigne looked past Doc. "What's keeping Raidah? Maybe we ought to go fetch him befoh he breaks the bastahd's neck."

"I told you, he's looking for the rest of the money."

"We can't take his money, Doc, we got no authorization."

He tapped the box held by the policeman beside him. "Of course, this is different, this contribution."

"For the last time, you gonna cough it up, or do I squeeze it outta you?"

"For the last time, you got all the money! Every penny!"

Doc came in. "Let's go, Rade."

"Go, shit! We gotta get the loot."

"Forget it."

"Are you loco!"

Doc explained. Raider listened, his shoulder sagging. Esposito listened, his smile widening, widening.

"Let's go," said Doc.

Raider grasped the door. "You go, I'll be right there. I just want one more minute."

"Rade . . ."

"Please, Doc, sixty little seconds."

"If you hurt him you'll be in deep trouble."

"I been there before."

He pushed Doc outside, then shut and bolted the door.

"You hear the man, cowboy? You can't arrest me. You can't touch me. I'm going home." He paused to check his watch. "Fifteen minutes we sail. You better get off, unless you want to go to Sicily, eh?" He laughed.

Raider glared. "I'm leaving, you bastard. But before I do, I gotta present for you." He stepped forward. Esposito cringed and backed against the wall. Light flashed in his hand. From nowhere he produced a knife, the blade gleaming menacingly.

"No, I gotta da presen' for you, Pink!" He moved toward Raider, swinging the blade back and forth. "I'ma fasta like a snake. I cut you open, let outta you guts, and when you faint from the pain, I carve a nice P on eacha cheek. P for Pink. You getta your picture inna da papers—dead. P P: Pinkerton Pig." He laughed evilly. "Atsa not bad, Pinkerton Pig."

He thrust forward. Raider sidestepped. The blade ripped through his sleeve; pain followed. Again the knife came at him. He saw red dripping from his wrist, dimming his gaze; saw red, his attacker's insideous leer, his lip curling. The knife flashed by. He grabbed Esposito's wrist. They closed, their faces inches apart, an inch. Gripping his wrist hard, Raider slowly brought it up between them, the knife point straight upward. Continuing to cling to the wrist, Raider closed his right hand over Esposito's right, keeping the blade in position, moving it slowly toward the little man's face. Esposito's dark eyes dilated with fear.

"No . . . !"

The point pricked his cheek. The carving began. Esposito screamed. Fists pounded the door. A shoulder slammed against it. Doc yelled. Raider ignored him. One cheek, then the other.

"D for Dulcie. M for Mae. Remember her? Friend o' yours, good friend, loyal, never had anything but good to say 'bout you. Loyal, straight. Here's a little something else for her. From her to you, delivered by me."

He powered a right straight to the jaw. Esposito's head, his cheeks crimsoned with blood, jerked back. Groaning softly, he slid down the wall to the floor, out cold.

"Son of a bitch!"

He picked him up by the hair and the seat of his pants and laid him facedown on the bed.

"Have a pleasant trip, you slimy bastard."

He patted him on the small of the back. And stiffened. Straightening his hand, he tested his back with his fingertips, pushing, exploring. He pulled up the little man's shirt. Strapped around Esposito's waist was a slender leather belt, securing a flat pouch.

CHAPTER TWENTY-ONE

The pelican's beak bag hung heavy with its catch. Raising its homely face, it gulped, sending the fish stomachward. Lowering its head, it eyed Doc through the office door. George sat opposite him, looking relaxed, rested, the beginnings of a new beard shadowing his face.

"When do you think Raider'll show?"

"He'll be along. He's gone to Emma Pickett's place on John Street to say good-bye to Billy Cobb. He'd better be along. We're supposed to leave on the eleven-thirty-six. We've got less than half an hour."

"Where you heading?"

"Denver. New assignment."

"You'll never get another like this one, right? What a crazy windup, you know? All that money strapped around his waist . . ."

"I told you before, it wasn't money, all it was was six pieces of double-folded paper. Six bearer bonds. Each worth one million dollars."

"And you had to go and give 'em to the mayor."

"For the city, George, for New Orleans. Can you think of a more deserving recipient? You put up with needless suffering, when it's cured, you're entitled to compensation."

"You coulda kept at least one for yourselves. Anybody just holding it in his hand can cash it."

A shadow fell across the desk. Raider stood at the door, bag in hand, blocking the sun. He came in.

"Hi-yah, George. Hello and good-bye. We gotta get moving, Doc. Billy sends her good-byes and says for you to take good care o' John O'Toole."

Doc nodded. "We were just talking about the bonds."

"Yeah, I didn't even know what they were. Never even seen one afore." He chuckled. "But we sure 'nough cleaned the bastard out, cash and bonds."

"Frank Montaigne sent a cablegram to the police in Messina," said Doc to George. "They'll be waiting for his nibs with a warm welcome. He's broke, he won't be able to bribe a soul. They want him for complicity in the murder of that minister, the Reverend Mr. Rose, the one they cut the ears off."

"They'll take good care o' old Espo," said Raider. "Private room, private bars, pet rats to keep him company." He studied his knuckles. "I give him a pretty good shot. He probably didn't wake up till that tub was halfway 'cross the Gulf o' Mexico."

"What do you think will happen to the first mate?" asked George.

"Him I kinda feel sorry for," said Raider. "Old Espo passed that money under his nose and his eyes fell outta his head. He'll probably get himself a few months. I feel sorry for his wife and kids."

"I don't think he'll get anything, Raider," said Doc airily. "More than likely he won't lose his job."

"Who says?"

"It's only an opinion, but if what he told me after you left us to go down to his cabin is true . . . Rade, Umberto Spallone is Captain Sebastian's brother-in-law. You know what blood is thicker than."

"He's a lucky bastard."

Doc had his watch out. He rose from his chair and picked up his suitcase. "George, I wish I could say it's been a pleasure. At least it hasn't been dull. Good-bye and good luck."

"The same to you two. Don't worry about luck with me. Business is booming, you know?"

They shook hands and left, walking toward the train station.

"Tell me something, Rade, now that we're leaving and probably won't ever come back, how do you feel about New Orleans?"

"Are you serious? It's the bottom o' the damn barrel! It's too cramped, too close, too many people, not 'nough air to go round, horseshit in the streets, dogshit on the sidewalks, water in the booze, fingers in the public trough up to the elbows, double-dealing, beaneries that clip you and poison you, the hospitals are damn butcher shops, every other shemale is a working girl, this wharf stinks worsen' a javalina..."

"All right, all right."

"All big cities stink. They got to. It's a law o' nature. Course, rats, stray cats, and dogs gotta have some place to live, and fleas, cockroaches, bedbugs, but that's what cities should be for. I mean purely. If people had any sense they'd clear out and go back to the farm. Another thing... Doc. Hey! DOC!"

Doc was suddenly walking faster and faster, getting well ahead of him, waving a farewell with his free hand and breaking into a trot. Anyone passing not seeing him wave would have assumed that he was fleeing dangerous company.

The last thing they would have imagined would be that he was simply getting out of earshot.

J.D. HARDIN

**"THE MOST EXCITING
WESTERN WRITER SINCE
LOUIS L'AMOUR"
—JAKE LOGAN**

JAKE LOGAN

Prices may be slightly higher in Canada.

Available at your local bookstore or return this form to:

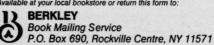

BERKLEY
Book Mailing Service
P.O. Box 690, Rockville Centre, NY 11571

Please send me the titles checked above. I enclose _____. Include 75¢ for postage and handling if one book is ordered; 25¢ per book for two or more not to exceed $1.75. California, Illinois, New York and Tennessee residents please add sales tax.

NAME_____

ADDRESS_____

CITY_____ STATE/ZIP_____

(allow six weeks for delivery)   **162b**